BLACK
ICE

TERESA LEE   **BRIAN WEBSTER**

WESTBOW
PRESS®
A DIVISION OF THOMAS NELSON
& ZONDERVAN

WestBow Press books may be ordered through
booksellers or by contacting:

WestBow Press
A Division of Thomas Nelson & Zondervan
1663 Liberty Drive
Bloomington, IN 47403
www.westbowpress.com
1 (866) 928-1240

ISBN: 978-1-5127-6455-0 (sc)
ISBN: 978-1-5127-6454-3 (e)

Library of Congress Control Number: 2016919120

Print information available on the last page.

WestBow Press rev. date: 01/19/2017

DEDICATION

To: **Christopher Webster**
Former Detroit Dragon
B.W.

To: **David, Blake, Tate, Drew, and Shane Schanski**
For their lifetime love of sports
T.L.S.

ACKNOWLEDGEMENTS

The authors wish to generously thank:

Deborah Mercer, Cathy Webster, and Ann Williams for their time in assisting as readers and editors. Our deepest gratitude, for your time and expertise in bringing the book to print.

A heartfelt thanks to our families for their support and encouragement along the way. The inspiration they provide for story lines, characters, and getting it done is immeasurable.

To my son, Christopher, thanks for hours of entertainment watching you play hockey with the Detroit Dragons. A big thanks to my wife Cathy for her support and encouragement, as well as hours of editing. BW

Thanks to my dearest husband and four incredible sons for the years of hard work and dedication you put into your sports. Your motivation to play, coach and persevere enriched my life with the thrill of the game, and the blessing of being a part of it all. Thanks too, for so generously tolerating my obsession with writing. TLS

Tremendous gratitude to the following for assisting in endorsements for Black Ice:

Tom Hunt, Athletic Director; East Lansing High School

Jeff Mitchell, OHL's Detroit Junior Red Wings, Former NHL Hockey Player; Los Angeles Kings and Dallas Stars, General Manager of Suburban Ice, East Lansing

Michael Krystyniak, YVS President/Superintendent Covenant House Academy

Maurice Dewey, Retired Lieutenant; Detroit Fire Department, Former Detroit Youth Hockey Coach

Our sincerest appreciation for the help and support of all those mentioned above.

CHAPTER ONE

I don't want to go home just yet. The sun is shining, and the sky is the bluest I've seen it in days. I am enjoying my skate to the max. With so many cloudy days in Michigan, any sunny day puts you in the mood to get outside and do something. Earlier I had asked Mom if I could go for an hour ride on my inline skates. She really didn't want me to go. I got the hint from her heavy sigh, but she is not denying me any request today. I'm not going to be gone too long because I know Mom will be waiting and wanting me to help out with the last-minute details before Dad gets home. It's one of those days that comes along once in every year and makes your heart feel twice its size. I just know the day is shaping up to be something special, but then it should be, since today is my birthday.

Born August 13, 1995, my name is Anthony Thomas Brooks, sometimes Shooter to my friends and family. My dad and Gramps gave me that nickname when I was about two years old. I had a fascination with basketballs, which I still do. I've had fourteen years of living in Detroit on the northwest side. It teaches you a lot of street-wise things. On my birthday, I guess it should be normal to think of all the things I'm thankful for in my life, and try not to dwell on the harder things we are going through right now. Our home is comfortable. It's nothing special, but better than some, built in the 1940s when all the car workers came to Detroit in mass numbers. Many Detroit families have been workers for the Ford Motor Company and made cars throughout their working lives. Mine is no exception.

My parents and I live in a two-story brick bungalow, like all the other tract housing on the block. It's a sturdy two-bedroom, which is just big enough for our family of three; Mom, Dad, and me. Gramps and Nana, Elmer and Cora Jones, moved to a bigger house a few blocks over when I was born. Our house doesn't need much paint, with the outside brick and the vinyl siding Dad put on around the windows and doors. Uncle Alonzo helped him with that job when I was about eight, to cut down on upkeep.

I enjoy hanging out with a few good friends. My best friend is James Ray Whitely. Generally life is pretty good if you mind your own business and stay away from the troublemakers. Avoid certain areas of town like troubled neighborhoods and usually things work out. Sometimes trouble has a way of finding you, even when you aren't looking for it. James and I are always on the look-out to be sure that we stay out of some peoples' way. Word gets around about that stuff. Today I'm not thinking of all that; in general, life seems pretty good on this sunny, August morning in Michigan. It is still cool, before the heat of the day. I'm thinking about my party later today and the presents I might be getting. It's certain: The skate is sure to be fine!

I'm counting on getting my own basketball rim with

a backstop for my birthday. Dad says when we get one, he'll attach it to the garage. He, Uncle Alonzo, and I will play some pickup games after school. Dad will keep the driveway shoveled so we can play late into the year, if it's not too cold. It is the only thing I asked for when Mom and Dad pressed me for my birthday wish-list. I saw the look on Dad's face when I told him what I wanted most of all. He had that determined crease above his eyebrow that he gets when he has a big project to get done. Yep, I know that look. He will get me my basketball rim. I just know it! Dad and Uncle Alonzo always take care of things.

Starting my skate, I am having more trouble than usual staying focused on navigating my way across the cracked, uneven, blacktopped surface that serves as the neighborhood basketball court. Even after the dry heat, the weeds are still sticking up. I keep my eyes on the biggest crevasses, choked with dandelions and small pieces of trash. I am heading for the sidewalk beyond, which borders the park just across the street from where I live. It is tricky maneuvering over all the junk sticking up through the broken blacktop, and jumping the big bumps in the sidewalk.

I make my usual mental checks in remembering to dodge the familiar hot-spots that have sidelined many a beginning skater. It's almost an unconscious, automatic habit now that I've learned where the worst of the challenges lie. I've had years of watching many skaters, inline and boarders, go down along this unforeseen obstacle course with nasty results. I've witnessed firsthand the havoc wrought when skaters with few skills have not been prepared for what this stretch of skating challenge dishes up. It has taken me eight years of practice, full of spills, scrapes and boxes of Band-Aids, to have finally mastered it. I usually have to jump, slightly air-borne, over the raised crests of cement slabs that form the walking route between the perimeter of the park and the old tree-lined street where I live. Decades of tree roots pushing up the cement squares of sidewalk in the oldest parts of town have created dangerous surfaces, a fact that makes for a very uneven ride.

More and more, when the cops aren't around, we just skate in the streets. My skateboard friends and I usually do our practice skates for speed, agility, and maneuverability at the free outdoor skate park in Hamtramck. It's just across the city limit line and a couple of miles over, but getting there on your skates or your board is the trick. Busy super highways you have to skate under, over, or around make it an even more dangerous task of getting there safely. Our moms usually just drive us.

I can't keep away the constant thoughts racing through my head about what my birthday present will be. Instead of going straight across the street toward home, I take one last ride down to the corner and back, just to feel the smooth flow of the street pavement beneath my skates. It's always best to end a morning trek on a smooth ride. Few neighbors are out this morning, so I have the street to myself, which makes the ride even more enjoyable. All the neighbors are used to seeing me fly by on my skates, so no one raises a head anymore. Today it's not the usual head-down wave and 'Be careful, Anthony,' as I shoot by their yards. I sail down the gentle slope of the street to the intersection, do a wide, lazy U-turn back for safety's sake, and head toward home. The breeze feels awesome, drying the tickly sweat beads streaming from my head and down my face. *Yes sir,* I think to myself, *it is going to be one great day!*

I skate up to the front of my house. I make a quick stop and sit down on our brick stoop. My fingers automatically unclip the three strap closures of my skates. Mom's rule has always been, "No skates on in the house!" My mind continues rolling: *My skates need replacing. I've had these Mach 20s a while. One of my favorite pairs of inlines, and I've had a few! First pair? Oh yes, Christmas, when I was six years old. Too big, but I grew into them quick. More pairs since then, but really these are starting to get too small and worn out! Money's tight right now. Man, has it already been a year since Dad and Uncle Alonzo have been out of work with the closing of the car plant? I won't be asking for skates any time soon, especially after I get my basketball backboard and rim. Don't matter anyway. I will be playing basketball, and won't have time to skate.*

It was an uneventful and enjoyable early morning skate. No one was about, bothering me or giving me reasons to be on guard. It was a great way to start my birthday celebration. I set my skates against the wood trim that outlines the front door, grab the door handle, pull it toward me and turn my house key in the lock. Just to be on the safe side, we always keep the door locked even when we are home. Can't be too careful in a big city.

The door opens on our small but comfortable living space. We have one sectional couch in dark brown, flanked on either side by two over-sized lounge chairs covered in suede print with various shades of green, cream, and beige in wide zigzag stripes. One chair for Mom and one for Dad, but Mom usually lets me sit in her chair and she takes the couch. We have a twenty-six inch Sony TV, which Dad and I spend as much time watching as possible. It occupies the center spot on the entertainment center against the wall that faces the couch.

I grab my skates from just outside the front door and place them on the black plastic tray that borders the linoleum-tiled entry floor. Just following the 'goes without saying' orders from Mom. Next, my shoes come off and get plopped on the tray beside my skates; also Mom's orders. The soft squish of the carpet under my socks feels good after the pounding vibrations of my skate, when I'm really flying. I walk stocking-footed across the brown shag carpet to the center of the room. I can't help but see a homemade banner hanging cross the room from one side to the other, that reads 'Happy Birthday, Anthony!' decorated in my favorite colors, navy blue, red, and white, the colors of the Detroit Pistons basketball team. Both Dad and I like the Pistons' colors because they are the same as the American flag.

"Looks good," I say out loud to myself with a big smile. "Yep, it's going to be a great day!" I continue talking to myself as I head for the back stairs.

"Anthony, is that you?" Mom calls out to me from the kitchen.

"I'll be back up in a minute. Have to change my shirt first," I reply as I start down the stairs to my basement bedroom.

"Well, make it snappy! Nana will be here soon, and I need your help with a few things," she reminds me.

I quickly strip off my Mr. Big Shot logo shirt, throw it in the clothes hamper, and grab my favorite Detroit

6

Piston's shirt from the bottom drawer. Before pulling it on, I head up the stairs to wash-up in the only bathroom in our house, on the first floor across from my parents' bedroom. We've all learned over the years how to survive with just the one bathroom between us. Some of my friends live in houses with two bathrooms or a bath and a half, which has only a stool and sink. Their families have more kids so they need it. Really, I don't know any other way, since I've never lived in any other house. I do know that Nana's nose never misses a thing. She would know if I had or hadn't washed after my morning of skate. I learned about her keen sense of smell a long time ago, sometimes the hard way. Nana made me go back to the bathroom and 'wash again' on several occasions. I don't test the waters on this one anymore.

"Where's Dad?" I ask out of breath, as I'd just run up the stairs two steps at a time. I stand, shirtless, watching my mother placing balloons around the room in various corners.

She keeps talking even with her back to me, "I sent him to the store for birthday candles, more than two hours ago! He said he had to run some other errands, but I can't imagine what is taking him so long! Everyone will be here soon," Mom finishes with exasperation. I continue my hurry down the hall to the bathroom. Nana would be arriving any minute.

I use the washcloth and give my face a good hard scrub to be sure no smidge of dirt could possibly stay put. My African American genetics look back at me from the mirror. Mom loves my shorter medium-length black curly hair and handsome looks. I always wish to be taller,

7

but neither, Mom or Dad, can claim legendary height as one of their physical attributes. I guess I will always be shorter than I would like to be, but there's nothing to be done about that. Dad and I lift weights in the basement for fun, so I'm proud of my body build. Honestly, I kind of like it when Mom and Aunt Cayleen tease me about my strong biceps and rippling six-pack. My legs are strong and muscular from all the inline skating I do, so overall I'm 'in good shape, with good looks to boot' or so Dad likes to say just to embarrass me. I can tell girls think I'm 'fine'. One of the older girls two doors down whistles when I skate by her house. Nana, my grandmother, doesn't care a dime about good looks and big muscles if I'm not clean, so really all that holds little weight around here. One last look in the mirror, a quick pic of my hair and …done. Hopefully Nana will approve.

Returning from the bathroom, and ready to face Nana's coming inspection with a smile, I see Mom still standing on a chair. She is putting the final touches to her decorations by sticking the last group of helium balloons to the wall with tape. Each balloon cluster is made up of the Detroit Pistons' team colors. It's a color combination that's hard to beat! I look at my mother working so hard to make my day special. I feel that funny lump starting in my throat, which comes when things touch your heart. Her back is to me, so she doesn't know I am watching her work. She turns to see me and flashes her big beautiful smile.

My mom, Michele Brooks, just never seems to change. She wears her thirty plus years well, and all my friends and family say she looks young for her age. Her dark brown eyes, big and beautiful, always peek out from under her honey-colored bangs. Mom's dark skin is smooth, with no wrinkles at all. She doesn't even seem to realize the way she carries her beauty off in such a noticeable way to others. She would do almost anything for me, and I know it. She always says to me, "'How proud you make me, Anthony!'" She makes me feel proud, too; both of my parents do.

I know I don't tell either of them how important they are to me. My parents can be tough sometimes. Both of them always expect me to do my best, but they have always put first whatever is best for me. Standing here looking at Mom, I can't imagine one day without them. They support whatever I want to try. Even though I am small for my fourteen years, standing at just five feet-two, I have never heard words like, 'You can't because…' come out of their mouths.

Mom gets down off the chair, and watches me walk slowly into the living room. "There you are, Anthony Thomas. You look great! I see you have on my favorite Piston's shirt!" She smiles again, as she carries the chair to the table.

"And mine. The room looks great all decorated. Thanks, Mom," I offer gratefully as I squeeze her around the neck.

"Oh mercy, you do smell good! You really are growin' up," she teases. "You best be watchin' out now, 'cuz Nana's goin' to get one sniff of you and she'll be laying kisses all over that handsome face. Mark my words! It's goin' to happen!" We both laugh at the picture that thought brings to our minds.

"I want to open my presents. I've been waiting almost all day," I protest. "Dad said I have to wait for the three of us to be together, before I can open my present. He said we would open it before the company comes for my party," I am playing all my cards, workin' hard to get my way.

"I know, I know, it is hard to be patient when you are thirteen," Mom smiles knowingly.

"Mom, I am not thirteen! I am fourteen!" I spew my ferocious counter to her remark.

"Oh, sorry; my mistake," she cringes visibly. "Technically you are not fourteen until 10:02 tonight. Besides, you know moms don't want their kids to grow up so fast. Wishful thinking, I guess," she quips.

I am not amused. "Well, I can't stay little forever! Besides, I'm not growing up fast enough as it is!" I retort, staring hard at my mother. At five feet, two inches I am probably the shortest guy in my class!

"That's why I've asked for a ....," I start to explain.

"I know... you want a basketball hoop for your birthday," she finishes for me.

"I figure if I could shoot like 'Mr. Big Shot', the other kids might ask me to be on their team. You know, Mom... shoot those last minute shots that win games? That's what I want to be able to do," I patiently reason.

"Mr. Big Shot?" Mom asks with a puzzled expression.

I pretend to dribble and shoot. I stop with amazement at her confused look.

"Mr. Big Shot, Mom. As in the poster drawings of him that Dad has hanging on the walls in the weight room? Chauncey Billups, best basketball player on the Detroit

Pistons team. Dad's favorite player and mine, 'Mr. Big Shot'. That's his nickname, on account of how he racks up those last minute points, just before the buzzer, to win the game. It always brings the house down! As Dad likes to say, 'Once a hero, always a hero.' That's how I want to shoot," I finish out of breath trying to get my points across. I pretend to dribble and shoot again.

"Well, 'Mr. Big Shot', now that you're getting older you should realize that money's tight right now, especially with your father being laid off," Mom reasons. "You know how hard it's been, Anthony."

I look away pretending to dribble and shoot. "Well, what about Uncle Alonzo? Can't they work something out together?" I continue.

"Your uncle doesn't have a job either, Anthony. You know that. No one wants it this way, but that's how it is since the car factory shut down and sent everyone home. Lots of people are really hurting," Mom takes a deep breath and tears start to form in her eyes.

I hate it when my mother cries! I feel so helpless. I don't say a word, but my sigh of disappointment is unmistakable.

She continues with effort, "So, if what you ask for isn't the present you get, remember that your dad is doing the best he can. He would do anything for you, Anthony. I am sure you know that, besides there's always… Christmas," she finishes quietly.

"It's not much fun, shooting baskets in the snow," I openly pout as I pick up one of my presents from the table. The table is covered with a decorated paper birthday tablecloth with basketballs all over it. The table

11

is scattered in cards and gifts. I pick up one of the larger wrapped gifts.

"Who is that present from?" Mom asks with interest.

"Uncle Alonzo! Can I open it?" I beg.

"I think it only polite for you to wait until he gets here," Mom says as she consults her watch, and I place the gift back on the table. Mom continues, "They shouldn't be much longer," comes her final answer as she heads for the back of the house.

I flop on the couch knowing this is going south fast!

"They?" I question, loud enough for her to hear me from the kitchen.

"Yes, they. Your father went to the store with your Uncle Alonzo earlier," she finishes, matching my raised voice, so I can hear her.

"Yes!" I shout as I bolt off the couch. "That must mean that he needs Uncle Alonzo to help carry the backboard and basketball hoop because it is too heavy for him to do it by himself! I knew it!!" I jump around shouting, "Yes!" to the top of my voice and moon-dancing toward the kitchen door.

"Anthony Brooks, calm down immediately! You're shaking the whole house! I wouldn't get my heart set on a basketball hoop," Mom counters seriously. She carries a chair over and reattaches a set of balloons that fell off the wall with my commotion.

"Well, I wouldn't expect you to get **your** heart set on a basketball hoop, Mom. But doesn't mean I can't," I smile at my own joke.

"Oh, you got me a good one, Anthony Brooks," she shot back smiling, too. "You're not thinkin' on gettin' too big for your britches now that you're fourteen, are you?" she pokes me in the ribs, and we both laugh.

I look at my name printed in black on the red, blue and white party banner she has up; just perfect. The waiting is getting to me.

"You said I could open a present before company gets here. It **is** my birthday," I beg again, determined to get my way in at least one thing on my favorite day of the year.

Mom nods her head in approval, as she looks at her watch again. The time for company to arrive is quickly approaching.

"Okay, then. Just one, since it **is** your birthday after all. I hope your uncle and Dad aren't upset because you just couldn't wait a minute more."

All smiles, I grab the biggest gift on the table and begin tearing off the wrapping paper and ribbon with a vengeance. The box told it all. My eyes open wide as I pull out a brand new pair of inline skates.

"A new set of wheels," I try hard to disguise my disappointment.

"Good thing I say, since yours are so beat up and getting too tight for your feet," Mom uses her most excited voice and wipes the sweat from her brow. "Nana gave Uncle Alonzo the idea. Wasn't that great?"

I look around. "Where is Nana?" I ask trying to change the subject of my disappointment. I was secretly hoping it to be a new basketball to go with my new hoop.

"Your dad and uncle are picking her up on their way home. She will be here soon," Mom informs me. "Nana's been putting the final touches on your birthday cake. As soon as your dad and uncle get back with the candles and

Nana, it'll be game time," Mom announces with an edge to her voice.

My eyes light up with anticipation. "Is she making my cake to look like a basketball?" I ask as I sit down on the couch for more waiting.

"Just what you ordered, Mr. Big Shot," Mom hints as my face breaks out in a smile. The room falls suddenly silent as I look at my mother intently, "I wish Gramps was still with us," I finish quietly.

With tears coming quickly to her eyes, Mom speaks barely above a whisper, "We all do, Anthony."

My cell starts buzzing. "Is that your father?" Mom asks even more impatiently as I lie down on the couch to check the call.

Glancing at my phone, I quickly answer Mom with a smile "James! He's wondering if I got a basketball hoop for my birthday."

"You could have invited him to your party. He **is** your best friend," Mom argues, starting with the same conversation we had the day before. I give her one of my 'Leave it alone, Mom' looks. I opted for a family celebration with maybe only James invited to join us. I know money is tight for Mom and Dad right now. A friends' party would cost way too much.

"He-had-to-stay-home-and-watch-his-little-brother-Jaden," I explain slowly, to emphasize the reason for James not being at my party.

"Okay! I'm just saying," she backs off with a shoulder shrug, and heads for the kitchen.

Before she reaches the kitchen door, the front door suddenly bangs open. In comes Aunt Cayleen with Nana, who happens to be carrying my birthday cake. Making for a grand entrance, Aunt Cayleen bows deeply toward me, as I am still on the couch. I'm like her kid, too and my Uncle Alonzo's. They don't have kids of their own yet, so I fill in. We both like it!

"Oh, for heaven's sake! I never even heard the car pull in the drive," Mom exclaims as she hurries forward to greet Nana, her mother, and Aunt Cayleen, her only sister. She gives each of them a welcoming hug.

"Here's one big cake, for one big Birthday Boy! Get over here and give your old Nana some sugar, Sugar!!" Nana finishes with her big deep laugh that seems to come from her toes.

I get up from the couch quicker than I mean to, after all I am fourteen now, and not a 'Big Birthday Boy!' That sounds so babyish to me. Still, I will never tire of the love my Nana shows me whenever she is near. She has always been my next best supporter in everything I try to do. My grandmother has reminded me many times, 'You will never be too big for the hugs and kisses your Mamma and Nana give you. Don't ever forget that!' She probably has said it at least five hundred times since I've been old enough to understand what she was saying. I do love her. Giving Nana commanded hugs is something I seldom mind doing: At least whenever I am not in front of my friends.

"It's a sweet cake, Nana!" I say to her as I stare down at the awesome cake she is still holding. She has made the cake into a huge basketball with my name in the Piston's team colors.

"Should be, I put enough sugar in it! Three whole

cups!" Nana says as she walks across the room and sets the cake on the table, turning toward me for her hug. I give her a big, full, two-arms-around-the-middle bear hug, which makes her laugh loud and long.

"Well, mercy me if this boy doesn't smell like Heaven itself!" Nana beams. "You is growing up to be a man, as sure as the sun comes up in the mornin'! Just don't be doin' it too fast!" she warns with a smile. Then just as Mom had predicted, Nana planted one big kiss right on my neck and hugged me tight around the middle. We all shared the moment of fun.

"Let's get this party started!" Aunt Cayleen calls from the hall.

"They're not here yet?" Nana demands breathlessly of my mother.

"Not yet, but should be any minute now," Mom defends.

"Where are those sons-in-law of mine?" Nana complains. "I finally had to give up on the idea of them coming to get me and called Cayleen to pick me up and bring me here. I knew you were busy and I sure wasn't missin' a minute of this party on account of those two bein' so late! I swear, I'm thinkin' they absolutely forgot about their own mother-in-law!" she finishes with a pout.

"How long they been gone, Michele?" Aunt Cayleen asks with a worried tone as she hangs her purse on the hook in the entry hall. "I talked to Alonzo at 11:30, and he said it wouldn't be long. That was two hours ago! Did they come back and then leave again?" Aunt Cayleen wants to know.

"No, I haven't seen them since they left here at 10:30.

Tom said they wouldn't be gone long, but had a few stops. Maybe they have a flat tire or something," Mom finishes with an increasingly tense tone to her voice.

The doorbell suddenly chimes. I shout from the couch, "Dad and Uncle Alonzo!"

I hear Mom let out a sigh of relief, "There they are, finally!" she states with irritation.

"About time those men got here," Nana complains again.

"I'll get the matches," Mom announces as she walks quickly toward the kitchen.

"Anthony, get the door please," my mother orders over her shoulder as she passes the couch.

"It's your birthday, Anthony. Sit down. I will get the door," Nana offers sweetly, still somewhat breathless. Aunt Cayleen walks over and sits down beside me on the couch. She pats my leg and smiles at me. We both watch as Nana goes to open the door. I think to myself...*Oh boy, Dad and Uncle Alonzo are gonna' hear about being late, but finally, the best part to a great day is about to begin!*

CHAPTER TWO

ana opens the door with a good pull, about to let Dad and Uncle Alonzo have it for being late. She stands motionless, staring out the doorway, not moving a muscle. Aunt Cayleen and I can't see who is at the door, because the living room wall partially blocks the view of the entry. Nana's strange silence, as she stares out the open door, causes Aunt Cayleen to stand up from the couch and start toward Nana. I hear Aunt Cayleen draw in her breath with alarm. I stand quickly and walk to the archway between the living room and the entry. Nana is standing face to face with two, younger, uniformed police officers looking very official, waiting on the front porch. Both are tall and big in stature, but clearly uncomfortable with what they are about to do. The two officers remain standing side by side. One of the men shifts his weight from one foot to the other, while his partner coughs.

"Uh Ma'am, is this the residence of Thomas A. Brooks?" the slightly older, tallest officer asks haltingly.

Nana's back is to me, but I can tell by the fear in her voice that she is scared, "It is," she answers weakly. "What business do you have with my son-in-law, Officer?" she asks placing her hands on her hips.

"Is there a Mrs. Thomas A. Brooks at home?" the same officer continues to press.

"There is," Nana replies without moving. Both the officers and Nana stare each other down.

"May we step in? We would like to speak with her," the other officer requests politely. " It's a little warm out here today, Ma'am. We'd be much obliged."

Nana moves back a step but not far enough to allow them to pass into the entry, as she quietly orders, "Cayleen, go to the kitchen and fetch Michele."

Aunt Cayleen passes me in the living room doorway and pulls my hand to follow her. All three of us almost collide as Mom comes from the kitchen, carrying the matches she had gone to get. Aunt Cayleen makes me stay with her as she looks at my mother with tears in her eyes.

"Michele, we got trouble. Go to the door with Ma," Aunt Cayleen's hands are trembling as she firmly holds me there with her. Aunt Cayleen pulls me to a position beside her where we both can see through the room to the door.

"What's this all about?" Mom asks with obvious fear in her voice, as she approaches the front door, seeing the cops. Nana remains standing there, still blocking the entrance.

"These officers want to talk to you, Michele," Nana states with uneasiness in her voice.

"Well, get out of the way, Mamma so they can come in," my mother orders Nana more gruffly than usual. The officers step over the threshold into the small, much cooler, dark entry way.

"Are you Mrs. Thomas Anthony Brooks?" Again the tallest officer speaks.

"I am. We're just about to celebrate my son's birthday," Mom offers. The two officers immediately take in the decorations that are hanging throughout our small bungalow. Both sets of eyes, surveying the room, come to rest directly on Aunt Cayleen and me. We are still standing stuck to our spot by the kitchen door. As their eyes fall on me, I feel a painful knot come into the pit of my stomach. Both policemen share uneasy glances and return their attention back to my mother.

"Can this wait until tomorrow? Is there a serious problem?" Mom asks with apprehension as both officers stand, staring at her silently.

"Ma'am, perhaps it would be best if you would step outside for a moment," the tallest officer offers quietly, glancing toward Aunt Cayleen and me.

"Whatever you have to say, can be said to all of us. There are no secrets in this house," Nana speaks with determination, as both officers stand in grim silence.

The two officers continue looking straight ahead. Nana steps up beside my mother and takes her hand. In the next moment the words come; the words which shatter all our lives. The tallest officer clears his throat uncomfortably before he speaks.

"Sorry to have to inform you of this, Ma'am but your husband, Thomas A. Brooks, passed away about two hours ago. It is with sincere regret that we have to tell you in this way," the officer concluded.

Aunt Cayleen slumps to the floor beside me, letting go of my hand. She is on her side, bent over wailing, with her knees pulled up to her chest. Her face is hidden between her chest and her upper arm. Her fingers are pushing into the carpeting and grabbing hold. The last words, streaming from the officer's mouth, sounded miles away and were drawn out in slow motion. I suddenly feel like I have to vomit. I run to the kitchen sink and throw up my breakfast. I slump down to the kitchen floor and try to squeeze my eyes tight shut to stop the tears from streaming down my face. I want the world to stop and rewind to the moments before Nana had opened the front door. I want to delete all that I had just heard. I could barely catch my breath. Am I even breathing? My mind is racing.

No! No! No! This can't be true! It just can't be. I know I will wake up and it will all have been a nightmare. Dad will come and tell me it is all right, and to just go back to sleep. No! No! Please let this not be true!

I jump up and puke again in the sink. Suddenly my eyes shoot open and all I can think of is my mother. I race out of the kitchen and run to where she is slumped on the floor. Nana is on her knees beside Mom holding her. Both are sobbing.

"How could this happen?! Where is he? What is going on? This can't be true!" my mother's questions tumble over each other, between sobs. Her feelings mirror mine, as she demands to know something, anything from the officers.

"It appears as if he was involved in robbing a local sporting goods store," the second officer explained, with obvious discomfort. Dead silence follows this revelation. Both officers are sweating heavily, with the perspiration running down the sides of their faces, from under their hats.

"I am sorry to say that a Mr. Thomas A. Brooks was allegedly shot by the owner of the store he was attempting to rob. Mr. Brooks expired at the scene. And the other man...," the officer stares down at the notepad he is holding in his hand. "The other man, a Mr. Alonzo Givens...," the officer repeats as he begins. Aunt Cayleen starts screaming from her position on the floor next to the kitchen doorway where she had collapsed. Paralyzed with grief and fear, she is inconsolable.

"What about him? He is my brother-in-law and her husband," Mom implores through her tearful sobs, pointing to Aunt Cayleen.

"Ma'am, I am so sorry to have to state all of this in front of your son," the officer hesitates, looking at my mother, as if hoping to be released from having to continue. Mom motions for him to finish.

"Mr. Givens is being held at the Detroit city jail, Third Precinct. He was not injured seriously. He is under arrest for the attempted robbery of Sammy's Sporting Goods store. Your husband and Mr. Givens appear to have been working together. Givens will be arraigned tomorrow at the earliest," the officer finishes looking sadly at me.

I am completely numb! It is like it is all happening to someone else, not me. I kneel down, placing my hand on my mother's shaking back. Nana and I help her to stand up on quivering legs. I try to support her as much as I possibly can.

"My Thomas? It **must** be someone else. It **has** to be. There's been a terrible mistake! He'd never do such

BLACK ICE

a thing! He would never steal from anyone, no matter what!" my mother reasons aloud with conviction in her defense of my dad. She is arguing half to herself and half to the officers. She keeps shaking her head 'no' over and over again. There is no making sense of this unbelievable story we've just been told by these black uniformed strangers.

"No, he wouldn't, Daughter! Exactly right, and that's a fact!" Nana states emphatically, holding tight to Mom. Nana continues to stare, with a protective glare, at the two officers, still unwilling players in this emotionally charged scene.

"Ma'am, the wallet on the body had a driver's license with the name of Thomas A. Brooks," the first policeman supplies sympathetically.

"Maybe someone stole it from him," Mom offers with expectant possibility.

"Ma'am, your husband was dead at the scene; shot by the store owner. Our squad responded within minutes. No one was allowed near the victim," the first officer explains, as he assists my mother's attempt to stand.

The second officer continues, "Ma'am, I am so sorry, but we ran the make of the truck left at the scene. The title of the vehicle belongs to Mr. Alonzo Givens. Did your husband leave home today in a 2000 silver, Ford F-150 truck driven by Mr. Givens?"

The officers' questions are tearing us all apart. Aunt Cayleen starts screaming again, still lying on the floor near the kitchen doorway. She is sobbing out of control, unable to even stand.

Mom's eyes start to fill with tears again, as the reality of what she had just heard was finally sinking in, "No,

Thomas! No, please! This can't be true!" Nana and I both reach for Mom as she collapses once again on the floor. There is no stopping the flood of her tears.

The two officers move quickly to support both Mom and Nana. They help them into the living room to sit on the couch. My hands are sweaty, my legs are shaking uncontrollably. Everyone is a mess! My whole life is instantly the worst mess of all! Suddenly, all I want to do is pound something, anything! I run into the living room to get away from my mother's visible heartbreak. Aunt Cayleen is still sobbing on the floor.

Without thinking I start screaming and tearing down all the balloons and the streamers. I tear at the banner as tears stream down my face. I run over to the cake which Nana had so carefully made for me with love and smash my fist into it over and over again. Frosting flies everywhere. When all that is left of it looks like a flattened mess, I slump to the floor sobbing uncontrollably. Cake is all over my presents, my cards, the table, the floor, and the walls. My life, my family, my birthday, will never be the same again. Not ever! At that moment, I hated my father.

CHAPTER THREE

66 **A**nthony, hurry up, we are going to be late. We have to be at the funeral home on time," Mom calls from the top of the basement stairs. "You've been down there all morning. What is taking you so long?" she finishes with impatience.

I had been drawing in my room, non-stop for over an hour. I was drawing my interpretation of a smoking gun: Morbid, right? I pull on my last shoe and tie the laces in a double knot. I check my tie in the mirror on the back of my closet door. A perfect knot with the tie hanging just the way Dad had taught me to do it. The top one slightly longer than the bottom one. My eyes start to fill with tears and I slam my fist into the closet door.

I grab my black, wool sport coat and head up the stairs in no particular hurry. *This day has to be the topper for the most miserable four days of my entire life! My dad, shot dead on August 13, my birthday, when I was still thirteen years old, but only by hours. Like Mom said, I had been born 'late evening' so technically I was still thirteen when my dad was killed. Had to know nuthin' good was comin' from that!* All I want to do right now is stay in my room, shut the door for the next hundred years or so, and pretend all of this never happened. I just want to draw my pictures for weeks on end, with no interruption. Maybe then, I can push all of this out of my mind. Maybe then, the movie of my dad getting shot will stop playing over and over in my head with no let up! Maybe then, I can escape into a made up world where everything is perfect and nothing bad ever happens!

Merciless thoughts keep on as I mount the last three stairs to the top landing at the funeral home. What is it going to be like to look at my dead father's face? I am barely holding it together, and the anger I feel is making my head throb. *How could he do this to us?! How could my father hurt my mother so completely? Who exactly is this person I thought 'walked on water' and never did anything wrong, not ever? How can anyone do such a thing to the people they love? What is everyone going to think and say about my father, the thief? How will Mom and I ever be able to go on without him? I don't want to be the man of the family, that role is his job. I will find a way to forget him. I will find a way to go on and he will never hurt me again: Never! I will prove to everyone that I am not like my father, and I never want to be.* I turn from the casket with no tears in my eyes. I feel like a cold stone is in the place where my heart is supposed to be.

Nana, Mom, Aunt Cayleen, and I are seated around my father's closed casket at the cemetery. Everyone, all our friends and family, dressed up in their Sunday best, trying to lend as much support and comfort as possible during such a difficult time. In the days leading up to my father's funeral, many people were coming by the house 'to pay their respects.' *Why are people paying their respects to a thief? What's worthy of respect there?* After all that had come down after the robbery, I was surprised at some of the good things that people had to say about my father. *How do you know if what you think you know*

*about him is the true Thomas A. Brooks, or the one who got shot
robbing a store?*

When Gramps died last year, November 29, 2008, it
was entirely different. Everyone was openly sympathetic,
and spoke at length about what a difference my Gramps,
Elmer Jones, had made in his living years. I was surprised
at the throngs of people who came to pay their respects.
My Gramps was always such a quiet guy. He worked
at the car factory, came home, went to work again and
again every day without complaint for forty-two years.
Gramps started work right out of high school at the Ford
Plant, on the assembly line, making cars. He was solid. He
never disappointed family and was always there whenever
anybody needed something, especially me.

Dad held us all up during the heartbreak of losing
Gramps. My grandfather was someone I had loved…close
to hero worship. Dad had made sure that everyone was all
right. He isn't here to do that now. He is never going be
here again. I have to keep telling myself that fact. None
of this seems real. It is proving to be a nightmare I never
wake from. Even when the sun is up and I am walking
around trying to seem normal, I'm far from that. Life will
never be normal again for any of us. I just can't figure how
my dad could do such a thing as rob someone. Dad and
Mom had always been so strict on doing right.

Countless people had come by the visitation for my
dad, but it wasn't like it had been with Gramps. Everyone
was quiet and uncomfortable this time, not knowing
exactly what to say. Some were really sad and in disbelief,
with tears in their eyes, even the men friends that my folks
had hung out with for so many years. Dad's men friends

tried to talk to me about what a great guy my dad was, but I knew they were lying. *How could 'a great guy' rob a store?* They told me how they'd come by to shoot hoops at the park with me. *Yah, right! I know you really won't.* Everyone talked to me about how my dad had loved all of his family, which was the biggest lie of all. *How does 'Love' do something like this to the ones who the 'Love' is supposed to protect?* The thoughts just keep coming.

I feel a stabbing pain in my chest, and my eyes start to fill with tears as they lower my father's casket into the ground. I can scarcely breathe, but I will not allow myself to cry. I won't let anyone see me break down over my father's death. I will never forgive him or Uncle Alonzo for what they have done to our family. *They don't have to listen to Mom's sobbing in the night, I do! They don't have to see the tension between Aunt Cayleen and Mom, I do! They don't have to watch Aunt Cayleen dissolve into a puddle of tears almost every time she sees me, I do.*

Mom and Aunt Cayleen are having a rough time getting along right now. They have always been open, sharing their sisterly love. They know everything that goes on in each other's life. Now, they are quiet with each other and tense. Never in all the days of my life, have they not gotten along, but a lot has changed since my birthday, when two uniformed police officers had come to our door.

Nana has been under the weather since the day after my father's death. She is at the house every day, to be there for Mom and Aunt Cayleen. Nana doesn't cry in front of any of us, but I can tell she has been cryin' somewhere 'cuz her eyes are puffy and red when she comes to the house. Nana had been feeling so poorly, she couldn't even make it to one of the evening visitations. She has been on the couch for the good part of every day since it all came down. I haven't slept a full night through in days. I spend most of my days skating or drawing. I avoid everyone as much as possible. I know that Mom is worrying about me, but I am worrying about everything now. Mostly, I am just plain furious! My fourteenth birthday was 'a game changer' all right!

I am never going to share another day of sports with my dad, Gramps or Uncle Alonzo; now that he'll be going to prison for years. I grew up instantly in only a moment. My hope, of getting a basketball backboard and hoop for my birthday, doesn't matter anymore. I could care less! Everything about living has become so suddenly complicated. All of life changed for each of us on that day, especially me. *Life in general is one stinking existence right now. Thanks, Dad!*

As soon as Mom stops in the driveway, I am out of the car and down the stairs into my room. I hear Mom calling to me from the car window, but her words are lost in my haste to be away and back in my own space. I close the door tightly behind me and lie down on my bed. I pull off my tie, and throw my black, funeral sport coat in a wad in the corner. I grab my sketchpad and start doodling. That's how most of my drawing goes. I just begin doodling and before I know it, the lines and circles start turning into something bigger than my original idea and more involved than I initially planned for it to be. Yep, the smoking gun was going to be like that, too!

Mom quietly knocks on my bedroom door. She comes in and sits down on the bed beside me. "Anthony, how can

I help you get through this?" Mom asks sympathetically. She reaches out and runs her hand down my arm, the way she did when I was much younger.

I can hear my voice screaming inside my head, but I don't speak a word out loud. *Really Mom? There's a way for getting through this? My dad was buried today! That adds up to one big game changer! Can't think of a thing I'd rather be doing on a Tuesday! How about you?* My mind races to reign in what I am really thinking and tone it down to a reply that Mom will find both appropriate and tolerable.

"I'm going to be fine. Mom, you don't need to worry about me. You are the one we should all worry about: You, Nana, and Aunt Cayleen. Nana hasn't felt good since my birthday and Aunt Cayleen seems like she's about to explode most of the time. Every time I see her she is crying, or has been," I counter.

Mom had become unusually quiet these days, especially when it came to talking with or about her sister. It was my turn to point out some observations, "Are you blaming Aunt Cayleen for Dad's death? It seems like you are feeling that she is responsible because Uncle Alonzo is her husband. She has nothing to do with Dad being dead! Aunt Cayleen would never do anything to hurt you, me or Nana. It's not her fault that Uncle Alonzo turned out to be such a loser!"

"Anthony, do not call your uncle a loser! I will not have you using disrespectful language about anyone! Especially, not toward someone who loves you very much! Uncle Alonzo does love you, and he always will. People make mistakes, sometimes very bad mistakes. Aunt Cayleen says he asks about you every day."

Since my uncle's arraignment, the day after his arrest, my aunt had gone to see him daily at the jail. Mom and Nana had refused to go. Aunt Cayleen never dared to raise the question... 'Why?'

"Oh yah, like he loved us so much that he robbed a local store so he could have...What?: A rap sheet, a felony record, a split family, five to fifteen years in the joint? He left you a widow and his only nephew fatherless! Yep, really shows how much **they** care...cared about us!" I let my anger speak for my heart.

Mom takes my chin in her hand, turning my face to look straight in her eyes. "Look at me, Anthony. Listen to my words," she commands.

I harden my heart so that no tears can come to my eyes. I try to think of something else. I focus on my anger. Mom continues holding my chin in her hand. If I stop looking directly at her, she stops talking and waits for my gaze to return to her face.

"Holding all this anger inside will hurt **you** more than anyone else. Come upstairs now and eat something. You need to eat. You need to be with the rest of us. It isn't good for you to shut yourself away down here and be by yourself all the time. You need to be with your family and friends," Mom ends her lecture to me. I pull her hand away from my face.

"What I need is to be left alone. Just let me deal with this in my own way. I don't like people telling me how I need to 'handle it', or what I should be doing. I will 'handle it' myself," I finish defiantly.

I can see the tears in Mom's eyes. I feel so bad for her and all that she is going through. I don't mean to be difficult, but I can't stand any of this! I know it has to be the same for her. I continue on, refocusing the attention to someone else.

"Nana has been sick since Saturday. Is she going to be okay with all this coming so soon after losing Gramps? I also know that you haven't been sleeping. I hear you up in the night," I add quickly trying to cover the weakness her tears always cause me to feel.

"Well, the only way you would know that, is if you are not sleeping either. This is hard on all of us, Anthony but we will figure it out together: You, me, Nana, and Aunt Cayleen," Mom promises. She rises to go and leave me in peace. She turns back at the door for one last directive to me, "Okay, Anthony. I will let you be for now, but I'm here whenever you need to talk, or ask me questions about your dad. If I see that you are not coming around soon, I won't let this rest. I love you very much. I won't allow you to shut yourself off from the world forever," with that Mom went out of my room and up the stairs. I fight the tears and win. I forcefully push my pencil to the paper and begin to draw.

After an hour or so, I am bored with drawing and decide to work out for a while. Down the hall from my basement bedroom, at the end of the furnace room, my dad had set up a weight lifting station for the two of us to exercise together. Since he had been laid off from his job, he used to work out when I was at school. He said it helped him to manage his stress about not working. I walk toward the weight bench, and to my surprise I see a big box setting under the shelf at the far end of the room. It is under the shelf where we always store the weights. I have never seen a big box like this one here before. It is wrapped with paper and has a large red bow on the top. I walk over to the wrapped box. I turn over the index-card tag attached to the bow to read it. It says:

To: Shooter, Happy Birthday, Son!
Here's to some great games ahead of us!
From: Dad and Mom, with love.

In anger, I start ripping the red bow viciously off from the top of the box, and tearing the paper off in a wild frenzy. I kick the box with the toe of my shoe until the box splits open. I see from the picture on the outside of the box that it is a Table Hockey Game. I grab the pieces out of the box and throw them against the wall of the basement. Nana and Mom come stumbling down the stairs into the room where I am tossing the pieces of the game around, standing over the busted up table, breathing heavily from the exertion.

"Anthony Brooks, what on earth is going on down here? Stop this at once!" Mom demands. She walks over to me and puts her arms around me, squeezing me in a tight hug. The tears start to sting my eyes, but I'm not giving in! "Anthony, Anthony, your father was a good man. You must know that," she continues to implore. I push her arms away from me.

"My father was a thief!" I yell at her. "I will never believe differently! He was shot robbing a store!!" My mother tries to reach out and take my hand, but I turn and head for the stairs.

As I'm going, I can hear Nana saying to her, "Let him

go, Baby. He has an aching heart. This is going to take some time."

I can hear Mom crying softly, "This is too much! First Gramps, now Tom. I just can't believe it. What are we going to do? How do we go on?"

"I know, Michele," Nana finishes sadly, choking back the tears as she begins softly reciting a verse from her daily Bible reading.

I hurry up the stairs, and sprint down the hall. I close the bathroom door and lock it. The tears flow unchecked down my face, wetting the front of my shirt and dripping onto the floor. I sit on the edge of the tub with my face in my hands. My body trembles with the effort to keep my sobs from being heard by everyone in the house. *I will never let anyone know that I cried for my dad. I will never let anyone know that my anger hurts this much. I want to scream my lungs out asking him, "How could you leave me like this?!"*

CHAPTER FOUR

I strap on my old, worn, slightly too short, rollerblades. I refuse to wear the ones that Alonzo Givens, my uncle, gave me for my birthday. I threw them in the trash. I think I could hear Mom fishing them out, but I haven't seen them since I deep-sixed them in the dumpster. *Don't want to either!* Next, I slide my backpack over my shoulders, and put on my headset. I pop in my ear buds and start the iPod. I've recorded and saved some of my favorite rap songs. The music starts playing through my earphones. I can feel it. This is going to be a better day. At least maybe not totally lousy like the last seven have been. It has been one long week since my birthday. I've been avoiding my friends and family as much as possible. It feels good to be moving again. Skating makes me feel more carefree like everything is more right with the world. *Right now, I could use that!*

I push off at a good clip, down the street that runs along the park. Here the neighborhood boys play pickup games of basketball on a cracked and weedy blacktop court with shredded basketball nets. The street is still quiet. Not many people about. I've got my wheels going and move with speed down the street. As I near the corner, I jump the curb and skid my wheels to an abrupt stop in front of a park bench facing the basketball court.

I plop myself down on the bench, take my backpack off, unzip the pouch where I keep my gym shoes, and pull out my basketball from the largest center pocket. I take off my rollerblades and stuff them into the backpack pocket where the basketball used to be. I put on my gym shoes, tie my laces in a double knot, and I'm ready to go. I drop my pack at the edge of the basketball court.

I pound the basketball on the rough, aging surface of the court. I am dribbling so hard, I can barely keep control of the ball. I shoot baskets hard at the backboard. Some go in, but not many. I mechanically go through the motions: dribble, dribble, dribble-shoot; and again, dribble, dribble, dribble-shoot. Suddenly, I hear the voice of my father whispering. It seems like he is standing just behind me.

His words come clearly to my ears, "Always stay focused." I turn and can't believe my eyes. I see a ghostly image of my father standing there, staring a hole right through me. His soft spoken words continue in my head, "Work hard, never quit and …," I turn away and shoot the ball hard toward the basket. The ball hits the backboard forcefully and ricochets back to me. "Always believe in yourself," my father's words just keep on. I dribble the ball hard against the slab of cement. I pound it to the pavement with a vengeance and the ball shoots above my head.

I shout as if to no one, "I'm not listening to you!" As I go up to shoot another basket, I whip around and fire the ball with all my strength at the image of my father. "Shut Up!"

Bam! The ball hits my best friend, James, squarely

in the chest. He doubles over in pain, gasping for breath. "Hey, Man!" James shouts and visibly grimaces as he stands up straight to face me, showing his full five foot seven inch height. He's still gasping, "I thought I might find you here, Shooter. Didn't think you'd try to disable me the first time you saw me!" James continues the struggle to catch his breath from my ball slam to his chest. I feel a world away, and don't reply immediately.

James and I have been friends since grade school. We are celebrating our fourteenth birthdays this year. We've been in the same classes for many years, and had lots of sleep-overs. We have a lot in common and spend the good part of every week together. We like the same kind of music. We both like to draw. We love the Pistons, and we watch out for each other: Always have, always will. He really is my best friend. It makes it doubly sweet that our moms are friends, too.

Mrs. Whitely, James' Mamma, has been to the house twice since the day my dad died, bringing food for all of us to eat. She has never been one for staying long, but both moms seem to enjoy each other's company. Mom, Nana, and Mrs. Whitely go into the kitchen whenever she comes for a visit. They whisper quietly over a cup of tea, share the latest neighborhood news, and then Mrs. Whitely leaves. After the most recent visit from Mrs. Whitely, Mom asked me if I wanted James to come for a visit yet. I didn't. I wasn't ready then. I wasn't sure if I was now.

James yells again, louder this time, "Hey, Shooter!"

I suddenly snap out of it. "Sorry, Dude!" I utter in shocked disbelief at what I had just done to my best friend. James pushes up his Harry Potter-style glasses to the bridge of his nose with his fingertips, and painfully attempts to straighten up. I jog quickly over to where James is almost now standing to his full height. "Sorry, I thought you were someone else," comes my feeble reply. "You okay, man? I guess I don't know my own strength," I finish with a sheepish grin.

James is finally able to talk in complete sentences. "I know you got a lot of business goin' down right now, but hey, don't kill your best friend. I heard what happened to your dad. Ma talked to your mom, and then to me. I'm really sorry, Shooter. More sorry than I can say. Been givin' you some time. The way it all came down, well that's as rough as it gets! You really okay, Anthony? You know I got your back, Bro!" James loyally vows.

I feel the anger begin to rise in my throat, my stomach, my whole body, and my head is throbbing! I dribble the ball away again, to keep the tears from coming, "Well really, how good can I be, James?" I shout across the basketball court. "My dad is dead! My stupid uncle is in jail, probably prison, for who knows how long?" I finish with a forceful slam of the ball on the pavement. I turn away and take a long flinging jump shot at the basket. The shot hits hard against the backboard and bounces off at an angle into the hands of a muscular, older, African-American teenager, who goes by the name of T.J. I know him well. The whole neighborhood knows him well.

James and I make it a habit to stay out of his way whenever possible. T.J., at age eighteen, has a reputation for being the neighborhood thug. He usually has a following wherever he goes, today was no different. T.J. has proven to be good at living up to his reputation.

"Hey, Shorty!" T.J. calls out, with an edge of disrespect in his voice. His buddies were all backing him, standing at close range. I look directly at T.J. ignoring the rest of the string-along gang. "Heard about ole' man Sammy taking out yo' pops. That's a call for revenge in my book, man!"

"Don't listen to him, Anthony!" James calls from his post on the other side of the court. T.J. turns his attention to James, glaring at him and pointing his finger threateningly.

"I swear not another word out yo' mouth or you got big trouble," T.J. warns menacingly. James shuts his mouth immediately. Bullies have that effect on people. T.J. takes me by the arm and pulls me aside as the others gather around. James holds his ground from the other side, but keeps his eyes squarely on me.

"How 'bout you getting ole' man Sammy back for taking out yo' daddy?" T.J. poses the question with a nasty grin on his face.

I swallow hard and pause a minute before I ask, "How?"

"Hit that dude where it hurts; his cash register," T.J. finishes with a low chuckle, at which everyone else standing around takes the cue and laughs, too. I wasn't laughing, in fact, I was beginning to sweat and feel very uncomfortable.

"Rob him?" comes my feeble and naïve sounding question. Everyone else starts laughing again, except James.

"'Is you stupid, or is you just plain dumb'?" T.J. ridicules with that all too familiar line from the movie, *"Remember the Titans."* He tosses the ball back to me with double arm force. It hits me hard in the stomach and I double over trying to catch my breath. All of his 'boys from the hood' laugh. "What ya' think I'm talkin' 'bout," T.J. sneers with determination. " I'll be getting' back to ya' soon," I knew for sure that was a promise he'd keep.

T. J. and his small band of supporters strut off the court. James and I hear their cutting laughter as they turn their backs and walk on down the block. I take a deep breath, and realize how badly my legs are shaking. My knees feel like they are about to give out. I bury my feelings and bounce the basketball hard on the court, beginning to dribble around in a circle to shake the weakness off. James jogs quickly over to where I am standing. I don't even look at him as I start to speak my piece.

"Nice that you could join the party, now that my booty isn't on the line here. So much for, 'I got your back, Bro'," I repeat James' words with a much angrier tone than I intend.

James jumps immediately to his own defense, "My eyes were on you the whole time. I was ready to join in if you needed me, but with those losers around, they would have beat me raw just for a laugh. I was more help to you just stayin' put!"

James knows the situation when it comes to this bunch. T.J.'s gang has a mean reputation, and anyone crossing them usually doesn't come out ahead. I know James' words are true, even though I am feeling miffed.

"What they sayin' to you about your business?" James presses.

"They sayin', 'maybe I should get even with ole'

Sammy for killin' my pop' that's what," I mimic T.J.'s words exactly.

"You don't be listenin' to talk like that, Shooter!" James implores.

"What d' you know about this, James? Your daddy ever been shot dead on the street?!" I ask with condescension.

"Well, I know for sure that your Mamma and Nana, and yah even your dad wouldn't hold with nuthin' like that goin' on! Your dad was a good guy, whether you believe it right now or not! That's what I know for sure!!" James finishes with a forceful shove to my shoulder! "You get your head straight, man!"

"Oh, you mean my old man that robbed a store, wouldn't hold with nothin' like me doin' somethin' illegal? Well, maybe you better think about that one again!" I turn my back on James, grab my backpack at the edge of the blacktop and head for the bench to take off my gym shoes and put my skates back on. *I need a good, fast skate just to clear my head of all this mess!!*

"I'll be by tomorrow, Shooter," James calls after my back.

"Whatever, dude! See ya' when I see ya'!" I'm playing the tough guy, but not enjoying it. I throw my bag on the bench so I can begin changing my gear. James gets that I need some space, and leaves me alone. I know in my heart that he cares about me, and is trying to be a friend in the best way he knows how. I'm just not there, and don't know when I will be.

I pull out my blades, stuffing my gym shoes and basketball in my bag. I grimace slightly, forcing my sweaty feet into my old skates. I quickly snap the latches tight, throw my backpack over my shoulder, and take off like a shot. This would be a long skate. I had a lot to think about! I know for sure that I don't want to see T.J. and his thugs anytime soon! I head away from the direction I had seen them go. *I know what my answer to T.J.'s suggestion should be, but I'm not sure what my answer to him will be.* The overcast sky matches my mood. The sun has disappeared and the clouds hang low in the sky. It is looking like it might rain. *So what? Let it! What do I care about a little rain?*

I walk in the door and set my skates in the tray, as Nana is finishing up setting the plates on the table for dinner. "Anthony, it is good that you are home just now. First, come and give your Nana some sugar, then get washed. Dinner will be ready in just a few minutes," she instructs. I reluctantly walk over and give Nana a peck on the cheek. "Well, is that the best you got today? My, my!" she protests with a chuckle and hugs me hard. "Your Ma only just walked in the door herself. Hurry up now."

I walk to the back of the house and down the hall to the bathroom. I turn on the faucets and look into the mirror. *I don't look any different, other than tired. Why do I feel so different? Something is different about me. The person I used to be seems lost or something, like temporarily gone.* I soap my hands good, rinse and wipe on the brown towel that hangs on the towel rack. I look into the mirror again.

"Hi Stranger," I say to my reflection in the mirror, "Who exactly are you? What's your name?" This was getting very weird. I turn off the light and shut the door on the way out.

Mom and Nana are already at the table when I walk into the living room. "Come and sit, Anthony. We are ready to eat," Mom orders politely, as she places the mashed potatoes in front of my plate. "James' mother brought over a cake and some ham today for our dinner. Wasn't that nice?" she asks with a listless tone. We all sit silently staring at the food. "Your dad loved this for dinner," Mom finishes with a quiver to her voice.

"Let's pray," Nana's words are not a request. We all bend our heads to pray and hold hands across the table. "Thank you, Lord for this food and all of our blessings. And, Lord we ask that you watch over our deceased loved ones in heaven. Good souls who were taken too soon. Also be with those of us here, who loved them so much. Help our hearts to heal. We ask in the name of Jesus. Amen." Mom and I repeat, "Amen," after Nana.

I open my eyes a slit and see my father's empty chair at the end of the table. Suddenly, without explanation, I just lose it. I kick my chair back and stomp out of the room following our, "Amen." The tail end of Nana's words, "Let him go, Child," are meant for my mother. As I breeze by Nana's chair she reaches for my mother's arm to stop her from leaving, as Mom stands to come after me.

CHAPTER FIVE

I didn't mean to kick over the chair at dinner. I was angry. I made my escape to my basement, bedroom dungeon to sulk. I had dozed off after drawing Detroit Piston's basketball players shooting, running, and dribbling the ball. I'd been drawing the Piston's logo on jerseys, and banners for over an hour. I had no idea how long I had been drifting in my dreams. My mind was thankfully coming back to a wakeful state with the familiar squeak of my bedroom door opening. It stirred me awake from the bad dream I had been having about T.J. and his band of troublemakers. I couldn't remember exactly what the nightmare was about, but I did recall my determination to escape. I had been speeding away on my inline skates, feeling afraid. I begin rubbing my eyes, glad to be fully awake, and look toward the door of my room to see Mom entering. I hadn't even heard her usual knock.

"Hey, sleepy head what have you been doing all evening? Looks like sleep will be coming hard tonight. How long have you been napping?" come Mom's queries as she crosses the room and sets a hot plate of food on my bed stand.

"Been asleep, maybe an hour or so," I groggily reply

after glancing at the alarm clock and the steaming plate of food.

Mom picks up one of the drawings that I had been working on before I dropped off to sleep. *I must admit that plate of food smells great!*

"This is amazing, Anthony! You are so good at sketching and drawing. Love the detail on the motion of shooting the basketball," she compliments.

"It's okay. The face of the player needs more work. You know, the head and the eyes," I argue. "Don't have that part right yet," I take the tablet from her, tear the page off with the drawing, crumple it up into a wad and shoot it towards the basketball rim that hangs on my closet door. "Thanks for makin' a plate," I finish as my eyes follow the paper wad as it falls through the net and drops into the wastebasket underneath it.

"Two points!" she adds, and then looks at me intently with her soft brown eyes. I know what is coming next. "Want to talk?" she asks quietly.

"Nope. Just want to be left alone," comes my matter-of-fact reply.

"Anthony, about dinner tonight," she starts.

"Yep, didn't really mean to kick the chair over. Don't want to hear Nana or anybody goin' on about what a great guy my dad was! Really? Robbing someone is okay? The worst is… he got himself killed doing it! Sure showed how much he cared about us with that one," I finish with disgust.

"Anthony, sometimes people have reasons for the things they do. Maybe not good reasons, but reasons. You and I both know your father. He would never have

45

done something like that unless he was desperate, or felt there was no other way out, or he got caught in the middle of something he had no control over. I want to know the answers, too!" Mom defends Dad.

"Yah, he got caught in the middle of something alright! He got caught in the middle of committing a felony and got shot for it," I snap back.

Mom ignores my angry tone and continues, "Maybe with time we will find out, and maybe we won't. What matters is that we have to hold on to what we knew your dad to be, before that horrible day when he was killed," she pleads.

"Well, what I know is this: With no thought of us, he did something even he would consider garbage! It cost him his life, and ruined ours! And, I'm done talking about this!" I say with conviction as my eyes start to fill with tears.

I stand up from my bed and cross to the basement window wall, in front of a desk that holds the framed picture of my dad and me on the basketball court. Mom had given it to me last year on Father's Day, to keep in my room. I tear the photo, ripping out the half with my dad's picture in it. I throw it on the floor, slamming the picture frame down on my desk to cover the torn half still remaining in the frame... me. Mom says nothing. Above my desk hangs an NBA poster of our favorite player for the Detroit Pistons, Chauncey Billups, 'Mr. Big Shot.' I don't look at Mom. I keep my back to her. I keep both eyes on the basketball, which Mr. Big Shot can be seen holding in the picture. I continue staring at the poster.

"Fine. I am always here when you want to talk," the

bedroom door closes softly on my mother's quiet words as she leaves. My cell phone goes off almost as soon as the door closes. It is James. I wonder, why the call, and not a text?

"Hey, how goes it?" James asks hesitantly.

"In general? Life stinks!" I answer my own question with conviction.

"Heard some guys are having a pickup game of hoop tomorrow, want to drop by and play a few games?" James presses.

"Why not? Got nothin' better to do. Sure. When?" I ask.

"After my mom gets home and I'm done watching my sister," James offers. "We can skate together from my place. Bring your gear."

"Okay, got it. Tomorrow then, bro. See you later," I push the button on my cell to disconnect.

Suddenly I'm feeling exhausted. I pick up the ripped off half of the photo from my bedroom floor and throw it in the bottom drawer of my desk. I flop down on my bed, dreading the sleepless night ahead.

The next morning, I wake up to a brighter day. The sun is shining, which always helps improve my mood. With all the tossing and turning last night, I was sure to run out of gas by mid-afternoon. At least I had a pickup game of basketball to look forward to later.

I arrive at James' house in the early afternoon. "So, who's playing hoops today?" I ask James.

"Probably the usual bunch. Hoping there are enough to get a good game going," James answers as he pushes hard on the top clip of his boots that locks him in and signals he is ready to go.

"After you, Magic," I tease as I stand up ready to go. He cracks a big smile for the first time in days. Things have been a bit strained between us lately. I haven't been into small talk and having company.

Magic Johnson is one of James' favorite professional basketball players. James' dad played with Magic Johnson for two years at Michigan State University. The two ex-Spartans still speak on the phone now and then. James loves that part. Ray Whitely dropped out of college after losing his youngest brother to a gang related killing in Detroit. Losing a brother had been devastating for the entire family and because of it James had an uncle he would never know. James' dad never went back to East Lansing, but he still loves the game of basketball, and keeps in touch with Magic.

We shoot hoops over at James' house most days of the week. We both really get into it when James' dad comes out and shoots around with us. James and I have gotten better at our own games just going up against Mr. Whitely. James is growing taller, towards having his father's height someday. At six feet and six inches, Ray Whitely is a force to be reckoned with, and a straight shooter. He plays in a city league most winters, and his team holds the city championship in basketball most years. So, basketball is one of the many things James and I enjoy together.

Today's skate over to the park proves to be three blocks of enjoyment. The breeze feels great to us as it cools us down. We don't talk much on the way over. A good sized group of guys are already there as we arrive. We sit down on the bench to pull off our skates and put on our gym shoes. Some of the neighborhood girls are milling around outside of the fence area which surrounds one end of the court. Whenever the girls are hanging around, it is almost certain that T.J. and his hoard are there, too. Most of the guys in sight stand taller than me, at least a good head and shoulders above what I measure up to in height. The captains are already starting to pick their players as James and I walk up, dropping our bulging backpacks next to the fence. James smiles at the girls. I turn to check out the situation of team captains and who is being chosen.

"I'll take Harry Potter on stilts, there," Davon orders, as he points to James. James reluctantly walks over to stand next to his new found team. Davon is one of T.J.'s guys. You rarely spot T.J. without Davon at his elbow. James looks at me with a, *'This isn't what I had planned on,'* expression. James and I always like being on the same team.

"I don't want that shrimp on my team!" the second captain complains as he points directly at me.

"Guess you're one guy short then, Manuel. C'mon, Shorty you can play on my team," T.J. puts his arm around my shoulder and leads me over to the side of the court where his team is standing, with Davon as Captain.

"By my count our teams are still even with that pick!" Manuel, Captain Number Two, crows with satisfaction.

T.J. gives him a 'Shut up or else' glare. "Hey, Beaner better shut yo' trap if ya' know what's good for ya'!" T.J. orders with contempt.

I can feel myself start to sweat, and I haven't even started playing ball yet.

The pickup hoop game starts and ends with bantering back and forth on both sides. In the end, our team comes out on top. The other team reluctantly concedes when the score becomes too stacked against them. The game ends surprisingly peaceful. James and I are sitting beside each other on the bench putting our basketball shoes into our backpacks and getting ready to put our skates back on. T.J. and Davon walk over to where we are sitting.

"Good game, Shorty. We clobbered those losers! You and your buddy there, Harry Potter, really helped us out today," Davon brags as some of the guys from T.J.'s gang gather around.

"James... my name is... James," James counters to Davon.

"Yah, well whatever you call yourself, you can play on our team anytime," Davon finishes with a smirk.

"So, what's on the docket for tonight, Hot Shots?" T.J. quizzes us.

"Going to Anthony's for dinner, in fact, heading there now," James adds quickly. I am totally surprised by this revelation, since I have no idea what he is talking about. We'd never discussed this option, but I'm not willing to blow James' cover.

"It's gettin' late. I don't mess with bein' late to dinner," I add quickly.

"You been givin' some brain mileage to what I laid on you the other day for gettin' even with Ole' Sammy for what he done to your pops? It ain't right lettin' a thing like that go without paybacks! We'll be in and out quick like! Won't even know what hit him!" T.J. snickers as he slaps his back pocket. Davon laughs like a hyena. Others standing around do the same.

"I'm still thinkin' on it," I answer truthfully.

"You listen to what I say to you, Shorty. He deserves bein' brought to his knees. Havin' his money swiped is one of the rightest ways to do it. Maybe when we're done payin' a visit to his cash register, he'll git our message and won't be shootin' anybody else's ole' man!" T.J. snorts with contempt.

"Me and T.J. got yer back, Brooks. You gotta prove you got ours," Davon finishes with a reach past T.J. and a poke to my chest.

"Tomorrow meet us at the four corners, across the street from the park. We'll be waitin' and don't be late. Kind'a like not bein' late to the table," T.J. laughs. Davon and all his homies laugh, too.

James and I skate away down the street, side by side, toward my house. We both pull off jumping the curbs to cross the streets. James never looks my way as he speaks sharply, "You jist get all those ideas out of your head! Don't be doin' no more to yer Mamma than's already been done to her. No good comes from listenin' to T.J.! He's filled up with hate for jis' 'bout everybody," James states with authority.

"Well, I think he's got the right idea about 'ole' man Sammy'. I think he ought to pay for shootin' my old man. Besides he'll still have his life, just not his money. That hurts people like him more than shootin' 'em!" I snap back.

James pulls up short at the start of the sidewalk leading to my house. He looks me hard in the eyes. "No good will come of this, Anthony. I'm tellin' you true as a friend. Stay away from T.J.," James begs.

"Well, since you invited yourself to dinner, you may as well come in and eat," I say with sarcasm, trying to lighten the mood.

"I'll be headin' home now. I've lost my appetite for eatin' thanks," James confesses. "Besides, that was just a cover."

"Why'd you say you were comin' to my place for dinner in the first place?" I question.

"I thought that was a sure way to get you home and away from T.J. and his stupid ideas. Those thugs he hangs out with are just like him; a low, mean bunch, all of them. Not like us, Anthony. We both know right from wrong!" with that James skates away toward home without looking back or waving good-bye.

CHAPTER SIX

I sail on my skates to the four corners. I skate up and down the block, jumping curbs, making quick circles around trash cans and benches, waiting to see if T.J., Davon, and the rest will show. It is about 7:00, and still no sign. I'm on edge, but keeping my nerves under control by skating it out.

I left the house after dinner with an excuse about meeting James to get a sketchpad that I needed for drawing. I told Mom it was my favorite one, and it was at James' house. She never even blinked at that, but then why would she? I rarely lie about anything to her, because I know what will happen if she finds out that I have. She is tough when it comes to lying. I'd been given the dish soap in the mouth treatment for lying when I was about six years old. I gagged and choked until I threw up! I've never lied much since then, only when I thought I had no other choice, and I was certain she wouldn't know. She would never find out about this, but I still didn't feel good about feeding her a story that was not true.

I spot T.J. and friends as they come around the corner. They are moving like a wave down the street towards me. I keep skating with my head down, not letting on that I've seen them. I pretend to be distracted, but am snatching glimpses whenever I can. T.J. is leading the pack as usual.

Also as usual, he is walking with his pants low around the top of his hips, with his baggy shirt pulled down long over the waist of his sagging jeans. His blue checked underwear is showing in spots, also usual. Both pant legs are worn and ripped at the bottom. He has a black bandana tied around his gray stocking cap, knotted at the back of his neck. A long silver chain hangs down over his short-sleeved t-shirt, which is covered by an open black vinyl vest. T.J. must think that his signature fashion statement is those black tennis shoes he always wears, with no laces in sight. They slop around on his feet as he walks. Whenever T.J. closes the distance between him and anyone, it is easy to see the nose piercing he has in his right nostril. A thick silver hoop runs right through it from the outside to the inside. T.J. likes to show off his arm tattoos, so he usually wears short-sleeved shirts, even in the winter.

James' older step-sister had dated a friend of T.J.'s a few years back. She told James some of the stories about T.J. He had dropped out of school about two years ago, when he was in his second year of high school. After that, T.J. lived out on the streets most of the time. His mother lives in a house near the overpass by the Ford Freeway, but T.J. isn't home much. James had said it was on account of his Mom's boyfriends. T.J. hated the way they came over, drank beer, and watched T.V. all day. His dad had been gone for about four years and T.J. rarely saw him.

I openly watch now as they cross the street, to let them know that I have seen them and am waiting. "Hey, Shorty what's up, bro?" T.J. asks cordially as he walks up to where I am standing. All of T.J.'s guys surround him. "Where's Harry Potter tonight?" he jokes. Everyone laughs.

"Don't know, don't care," I say, telling my second lie, and trying to sound tough. My nerves are really starting to get to me.

"You ready to show us what you're made of, and that you want paybacks for your dad?" Davon prods. "What you gonna' do with those skates on? That's a disaster waiting to happen!" he finishes looking down at my feet for affect.

"No need to worry about me when I'm on my wheels. I can skate faster than you can run!" I counter. Everybody laughs except Davon.

"Well, maybe we should have a race," T.J. offers slapping Davon on his back. "Or better yet, let's just see who is the fastest when things get hot! Come on, boys. It's time to lay Goliath low!" T.J. turns on his heel and starts back the way they had come.

I follow along on my skates behind T.J. and his buddies. We walk about three blocks from the park. T.J. walks into an alley near a city parking lot. He motions for me and Davon to come over by him and for everyone else to get out of sight. We three crouch behind a parked car in the lot. He points across the side street to Joe's Pizzeria.

"Joe's Pizzeria?" I whisper. T.J. nods. "I thought you said we were robbing Sammy's store?" I could feel the panic start to rise as I realize what his plan may be.

"We goin' to do that, too. All in good time, but first we have to initiate you into our club," T.J. grins and continues. "We gotta know you can be trusted. So, this is how it's goin' to roll. You go inside and order a pizza," T.J. explains as I listen carefully to the details. "When he opens the register, you goin' to grab the cash, throw it into this sack…," T.J. hands me a pillowcase which had been tucked under his long shirt in the waist of his low riding pants. There are no smiles now, only urgent commands.

"And…Run!" he emphasizes by clenching his teeth.

"What if he comes after me?" I ask with some hesitation.

T.J. emits a low sneering laugh. "Not to worry, Lil' Man. He's old and he got a limp. You'll be movin' faster on wheels than he can on heels!" Davon follows this last comment of T.J.'s with his familiar hyena laugh for emphasis and support. I exhale nervously and take another deep breath because I feel like I can't breathe.

"We'll meet in the ally right behind the store, where the other guys are staying put," T.J. commands. I shove the pillowcase into my back pocket, pull my jacket down over it and start rollerblading toward Joe's Pizzeria. I push the thoughts of my mom and James from my head each time they threaten to pop up again. I take another deep breath. *I have to do this.*

I open the door to the pizzeria and roll up the slight incline into the store. I slowly maneuver past rows of tables covered with red and white vinyl tablecloths. I check out Joe's Pizzeria. The place is full of hockey memorabilia: sticks, pucks, trophies, pictures, and banners. There are also autographed, framed hockey jerseys hanging on all the walls: Hockey jerseys belonging to very famous professional players. Some famous players are shown in photos framed on the walls. NHL players I had heard about and even seen on T.V. are looking out at me from the framed photographs.

A few customers seated about are talking quietly

and eating pizza. No one appears to notice me looking around at all the hockey stuff on the walls. Something seems very familiar to me about this place. I suddenly remember coming here with my dad once or twice when I was younger. We had ordered pizza and taken it home to share with Mom. Dad had talked with the owner guy quite a while during our wait for the pizza. Dad and this pizzeria guy had gone to high school together. Now, with trepidation, it is all coming back, as I remember why it seems so familiar. Suddenly, I start having second thoughts about what I am about to do. I fight the feeling and roll up to the counter to place my order.

"Yes, young man what can I do for you today?" the guy behind the counter asks cordially. I can't even speak and so say nothing. "What can I get ya?" the guy repeats patiently. *Must be Joe. Say something!*

I gaze up at the chalk-written store menu, trying to disguise the awkward moment. The big board of order choices uses catchy hockey terms for names of entrees and menu items like Power Play, Face-Off, and Slap Shot, to name a few. The menu is framed in hockey sticks that hang above the window opening connected to the kitchen. I have no idea what is coming next. I'm trying to stay calm. I'm trying to act normal and not tip him off.

"You been here to Joe's before?" the middle-aged dude asks.

He looks a few years older than my parents, but isn't old. He is short and stocky with a silver-capped tooth and a deep scar above his right eye. I see a few gray hairs showing at the temples where his head of black curly hair frames his face. His nose looks like it has been broken sometime long ago. It lays flatter to his face than most noses, and has a visible and slightly crooked bump up high near his eyes. When Joe walks from the kitchen doorway up to the counter, I notice the slight limp that T.J. had mentioned. *I could beat him easy, any day, on my skates. No worries about getting away from him,* I think to myself, trying to settle my nerves.

"Hey, Uncle Joe want me to get this one?" A pretty girl in her early teens walks up behind Joe and stands beside him at the counter. Both of them look directly at me, waiting. *Yep, it's Joe all right,* my mind is racing.

"I um… like to order," I stammer looking back at the pizzeria girl, then to the menu.

"Your 'um…Hat Trick," I finish. The girl looks at me and smiles. Joe scribbles on his order pad.

"The three meat pizza; my favorite, right Uncle Joe?" she smiles in response, and heads to the kitchen.

The guy looks directly at me, "Ten-fifty," Joe presses the key and Click! The drawer opens with the cash. Just then, the phone rings. Joe turns to answer the phone; just the break I need.

In the flash of an instant I reach over the counter, grab the money out of the cash register, and in a panic begin shoving it into the pillowcase as fast as I can. Joe is still talking and has his back to me. The girl is still in the kitchen. I hear the cowbell ring above the front door. I turn to see who's just come in, continuing to stuff the makeshift bag with handfuls of bills. *Oh no!*

A full-bodied, tall police officer walks into the pizzeria. It takes him only an instant to size up the situation.

"Hey!" he yells with a booming voice.

I bolt out the back with the police officer in hot pursuit. Even on my skates, this guy is fast!

"Get him, Bernie!" Joe yells after us from the back door.

"Dad!" I hear the young girl scream as I shoot down the alleyway leading from the back street exit.

"Stop!" the police officer yells. I can hear him pounding the pavement just behind me. I am weaving in and out of trash cans, around dumpsters, and under low hanging fire escapes.

"Stop! Police!" he shouts even louder as I speed around the corner down another connecting alley. T.J. pops up from behind a dumpster. I throw him the sack and keep on skating. Suddenly, only about three doors down, the alley narrows and there is nowhere to go except back the way I had just come. I am face to face with a dead end and a hard brick wall. I realize that I am in big trouble: Trouble that isn't going away. The officer turns the corner and I can hear his pounding steps slowing. He knows very well that there is no place else for me to run. I stop and put both hands up on the wall.

"I said 'STOP!' Turn around slowly, with your hands over your head," Bernie, the police officer, gritted between his teeth. He was out of breath and breathing hard with each word from his mouth.

"Do as I say and no one will get hurt," he continues. I put my hands up into the air and turn around slowly. My heart feels like it could fly out of my mouth. I am sweating like crazy, and my mouth feels like I haven't had a drink of water in years! I am really scared! I turn around slowly and stand face to face with the same police officer who had come into the pizzeria. He is still breathing heavily, but in control. Beads of sweat roll down his face as he stands with his hand fingering his still holstered gun, staring without a blink, directly at me.

"Young man, you are under arrest. Walk toward me slowly and don't do anything stupid. There is no way you are getting past me, so make this easier on both of us. I really don't want to have to pull my weapon."

I do as I'm told. There is nothing else to be done. When I am a few feet from the officer he holds up one hand with his palm facing me.

"Stop. Put your hands behind your back. Now, move slowly backward toward me," he orders.

I do it just the way he says. I am too scared to do anything else. I flinch when he snaps the cuffs shut on both my wrists. They are tight, and it hurts. Suddenly tears come to my eyes. I fight them, but this time they won't stop. I hang my head, and the image of my mother's face swims behind my tears. When we reach the police car, there is another one waiting at the curb in front of Joe's Pizzeria with its lights flashing brightly. A crowd is gathering to see what is going on. Officer Bernie pushes me up against the police car with my face against the back door frame. The guy from the pizzeria has come out to stand on the sidewalk, watching the interrogation.

"What's your name, kid? Where do you live?" Bernie asks sternly. I mumble my name low into the side of the car. The officer turns me around to face him and orders, "Speak up when I ask you these questions,"

"My name's Anthony Brooks. I live at 3456 Jenison Street," I snap.

The pretty girl, with the wavy black hair and friendly smile, who had been behind the counter when I walked in to order the pizza, follows the old guy out of the store and is standing there too, staring at me with pure contempt.

"Who do you live with?" Bernie continues prodding and scribbling notes on a clipboard he has just pulled from the front seat of the cruiser.

"I live with my mother, Michele Brooks," I answer weakly.

"Where's your dad live?" Bernie continues prying.

"My dad's dead!" comes my strained response through clenched teeth.

"How long?" he persists.

"About two weeks, if it matters. Got shot robbing a store five blocks from here," I spew out angrily.

Officer Bernie stops scribbling on his clipboard pad, looks up slowly, and stares straight at me. Suddenly, he seems to have no more questions.

"You Tom Brooks' kid?" Joe asks with surprise as he glances at Officer Bernie and looks me over like I am some kind of a bug.

"Yah, what's it to you?" I ask with anger.

"Used to know your dad some, that's all. Too bad about him," Joe says with regret in his voice.

"Yah, well as they say, 'Like father, like son'," I sneer with contempt.

The pizzeria guy looks at me long and hard, then he says, "I'm sure both are true, son. In which case, you are not close to being as bad as you are pretending to be." Joe, shaking his head, sighs deeply and turns back to re-enter his pizzeria. His response leaves me totally confused.

"Yah, that's right and don't call me Son! You're not my dad! I don't have a dad!" I shout angrily at Joe's back as he turns away.

"Pipe down and get in the car!" Officer Bernie commands as he opens the back door. He pushes my head down as I get into the backseat and says, "My brother Joe there, speaks true. So what **are** you doing sitting in the back of my police car right now?"

He locks the door behind me with his remote key. The officer from the other squad car stands guard while Bernie the Badge goes into the pizzeria to take the report from Joe the Pizzeria guy. I am relieved to be in the car at last, so everyone stops staring at me like I am some space alien. *Never would have guessed the pizza guy and cop as brothers.*

From my position in the backseat of the police car, I scope out the surrounding area. There is no sign of T.J. anywhere to be seen. He must have taken off from his hiding place behind the dumpster when the officer ran past him. There is no sign of the guys who had tagged along through all of it; waiting in the parking lot across the street from the alleyway where it all went down. There is only my mother's face, James' words of warning, and my Nana's eyes filled with love only for me, swirling in my mind. My heart becomes heavier with each tick of the clock, as I sit in the back of a city of Detroit police car and wait for the next thing to happen.

CHAPTER SEVEN

M ichele Brooks finds herself walking nervously from the couch to the dining room table and back again. Anthony had been gone for over two hours. It had been dark for over an hour. What was it that he had said before he hurried out the door? She was going over and over it in her mind, letting her words speak her questions aloud. It was something about meeting James, and getting a notebook for drawing. She had called her mother and checked with Cayleen to see if he had skated over there. No Anthony. Michele walks about the house, nervously dialing the Whitely home on her cell phone.

"Hi Arlena, this is Michele Brooks, is James there? I would like to speak with him for a minute please," she asks trying not to sound alarmed. Michele can hear Arlena calling for James to come to the phone. Michele is sweating.

"Hello, Ms. Brooks," James greets respectfully.

"Hi there, James. Were you with Anthony earlier this evening?"

"No, Ms. Brooks why you asking me that?" James questions with a catch in his voice.

"Well, Anthony told me that he had left his sketchpad at your house, so he was going to meet you and get it," silence follows on the other end of the phone. "Did you meet him, James? Did Anthony come to your house for the sketchpad?" Michele grills James with her questions.

"No, Ma'am. I didn't meet or see Anthony tonight," James shares truthfully. "But I think I might know where he is," James offers quietly. "I been real worried about Anthony, Mrs. Brooks."

James goes on to tell Michele about the conversation that had gone on at the park earlier that day, and about the talk that was shared the last time Anthony had met T.J. at the park. Michele listens to James share his concerns about Anthony, "I been tellin' him for days not to be bendin' his ear to what that loser T.J. has to say... 'bout gettin' even with Sammy for what happened to his dad," Michele's heart feels like it is in her throat. She can scarcely breathe with the words she is hearing from James. James finishes by telling her that he and his mom are coming right over to help.

"Just a minute, James. Someone is at the door. I have to go, but please come over as soon as you can. I think you can help me," Michele finishes with urgency.

"Be right there, Mrs. Brooks," come James' final words as Michele hangs up the phone.

Michele walks quickly to the front door to answer the third knock. When Michele Brooks opens the front door and sees the two police officers standing there, she completely loses it. She dissolves into a puddle of tears and weak knees on the floor. It has taken several minutes of steady talking by the police officers for it to sink into her mind that Anthony is not harmed; in fact, that he is very much alive, but in some serious trouble.

Momentarily, James and his mother arrive on this scene. Arlena calls Michele's mother and sister. They come flying into the drive only minutes later, with Cayleen behind the wheel. Everyone is in shock at the turn of events as they relate to Anthony.

"There's no chance of Anthony doin' such a thing!" Nana laments after the officers had left. "It just can't be so!"

"Well, it is so, Ma! And all that is to be done now is to show up at the court house tomorrow at 11:00 like the officers told us to do. We can see Anthony then and not before. Maybe a night in juvenile custody will get him thinking straight again!"

They all knew there would be little sleep this night for anyone. "How can they keep a young boy like that from his Mamma?" Cayleen continues questioning with a teary voice.

The police told Michele that she would not be able to see Anthony until the next day. The arresting officer shared that Anthony would be taken to Juvenile Detention and the arraignment would be in court the next day.

"Well, I guess this is better than jail, but it still is not looking good for Anthony. I hope he is good and scared, cuz' he should be! Life's been rough, losing his dad and all, but even that is **no** reason for him to be doin' such things!" Michele spewed in anger. Now that she had fully recovered from her fear of Anthony being seriously hurt or dead, she was furious with her son's behavior.

"James, do you have any idea who else might be involved?" Nana asks with intense interest. "The police are saying the money that Anthony stole is nowhere to be found. They searched that alley from top to bottom; nothing, and it wasn't found on Anthony when he was caught," Nana reasons trying to put together the pieces of this unexpected puzzle.

"There has to be someone else involved. There has to be someone else who put him up to this," Cayleen insists. "Everyone, who knows Anthony, knows he would never do something like this! The police felt certain that others were involved, but didn't know who," she debated.

It was Arlena, James' mother, starting in next, "Please, James if you know anything about this you must share it with us. Anthony's family needs to know what exactly or who exactly is in the middle of all this. We will figure out the best thing to do, together." Mrs. Whitely continues pleading with her son, "Do I need to call your father to come over here?"

"Mom, the people involved are dangerous. You don't want to mess with T.J. and his pack. They do bad stuff, sometimes really bad stuff! They aren't afraid of anyone, not even the police. If I snitch on them to the police, they will come after me and maybe even you, Dad, Jaden, and Ameika," James desperately tries to explain. "I'm not willing to take a chance like that," James finishes with determination.

"James, please trust us. They will not know that you told the police anything," Michele vows. "I will make sure of it."

"We will all make sure of it!" Nana finishes with a firm set to her jaw.

CHAPTER EIGHT

*M*ichele, Nana, and Cayleen arrive at the courthouse at 11:00. The hearing is to be held in thirty minutes. Michele has not slept a wink all night. She is about to see Anthony for the first time, since he left the house last night. She is trembling from nerves, lack of sleep, and trepidation for what might happen to her son. She met briefly with Anthony's attorney, Mr. Jack Arnett, just after arriving at the court house. He asked her some pointed questions about Anthony, the family situation, and her take on all of this. She answered him honestly and begged for him to do whatever possible to help her son.

"What is the number of the courtroom we're supposed to go to for the hearing?" Nana asks for the second time.

"Courtroom four, Mamma. That's what the clerk at the front desk told us. That's where Anthony will be arraigned," Cayleen repeats again.

"Let's get this over with," Michele sighs. She takes her sister's hand on one side and her mother's on the other. They walk together toward the courtroom marked with a number four above the door.

Michele feels as though her legs will not carry her when she sees her son sitting dejectedly at the defendant's table alongside his court-appointed attorney, a middle-aged man in a crisp white shirt, a stylish tie, and a double-breasted suit coat.

Anthony's family of three take a seat four rows back behind where Anthony is sitting. All attention soon focuses on the judge seated behind the bench at the front of the courtroom. They are trying to discern his mood, or his temperament. He is older, robust, bald, and wearing glasses. It also doesn't help that he is white.

"I think he looks like Anthony's big, fat, furry, two-eyed basketball!" Cayleen bends over and whispers ever so quietly to her sister, referring to one of the stuffed toys that had been a favorite of Anthony's since he was small.

"I hope he has grandchildren," Nana wishes in a hushed voice.

"I just pray the Good Lord is lookin' down on us today, and that Tom and Dad are puttin' in the best they got to say about our Anthony," Michele finishes through tears. "Mamma, you know the verse from St. Matthew, Chapter 21; verse 22…? 'Whatever you ask for in prayer with faith, you will receive.' Well, I'm askin' with every ounce of faith I got!" Michele wipes away more of her tears.

Anthony's Day in Court

I hear the key turn in the lock to the small cramped room, with a single cot, where I stayed last night. One little window with bars over it is the only outside light in the room. The side wall lights are off. I am lying on the cot looking at the ceiling. My mind has not been at rest all night.

A police officer opens the door and stands aside. My

court-appointed attorney walks in followed by an assistant carrying a bulging notebook and pen. The police officer stays by the door. I'm really tired. My stomach is growling, but I'm not hungry. I feel sick and shaky. The attorney guy starts right in grilling me.

"Hello, Anthony. I'm Jack Arnett, your attorney and this is my assistant Jason Rymes." The guy nods in my direction, as my attorney continues.

"If I'm going to defend you in this case, you have to be straight with me. Tell me exactly what went down and how," Mr. Arnett insists with authority as the assistant scribbles notes furiously in his very official notebook.

"Yes Sir, Mr. Arnett I'll be tryin' to do that," I answer sullenly. This Mr. Arnett seems okay. One of those typical highly educated guys who thinks they know it all, but don't. You just got to roll with them.

"Anthony, did you rob the cash register in Joe's Pizzeria?" my attorney asks plainly but with authority.

"Yes Sir, I did," I say looking around the room at the ceiling.

"Look at me when I speak to you. Did you act alone?" he persists.

"Kind of... yes," I reply looking him straight in the eye.

"Were you forced to commit the robbery, and by that I mean was anyone coming down on you with threats, so you would take the money?"

Glancing out the window across from where I was sitting I say, "No," even though I know it isn't all together true. *Snitching on T.J. is only going to get me into more trouble.*

"So, Anthony look at me. Where's the sack of money?" Mr. Arnett continues to press.

"Don't have the least idea," I say kind of truthfully.

"That's obvious, since it wasn't in your possession at the time of your apprehension, and the arresting officers scoured the alleys up, down, and sideways. So, who snagged the bag, so to speak?" Mr. Jack Arnett wasn't cutting me any slack in letting me off with my answer. Surprisingly, this guy seems to know the score.

"I don't remember, some guy in the alley, maybe," I evade.

"What? You dropped the bag? You tossed it in a dumpster? Some guy just happened to find it laying around? Come on, Anthony! Look at me!" Jack Arnett slams his fist on the table. I jump with surprise.

Mr. Arnett continues, "What went down? If you want me to keep you from breaking your mother's heart, come clean with me!" He was hitting below the belt bringing Mom into it. Tears were threatening to start. I feel tired and so confused. I feel my determination starting to weaken. *What am I even doing sitting in a courthouse across the table from some guy who is trying to keep me out of a juvenile detention home. Why did it all have to go so wrong?*

Sometime later, a police officer leads me into the courtroom with Mr. Jack Arnett and his assistant following behind. At least I don't have to wear handcuffs into the courtroom. Those have a way of really making you feel like a low life. I am relieved to see that Mom and Nana haven't arrived yet, so I won't have to face them as I walk in, on my way to the defendant's table. I feel thankful that Mom won't have to see me led in, handcuffed.

Faces I do see and recognize when I enter the courtroom are the pizza guy, the girl behind the pizza counter, and the police officer who arrested me, Bernie. He is in his uniform, so I know he will probably be testifying against me. I look immediately down at the floor, because… if looks could kill, that middle school girl with the black wavy hair would have already committed murder on me! The court police officer motions for me to sit. My attorney and the scribbler come to sit on each side of me. I keep my eyes looking straight ahead, facing the judge's bench. At least my back is to the people seated in the courtroom. I won't have to look at my mother's face. The judge is already sitting there, reading papers or something and looking down totally zoned out, as if no one else is even in the room. This is getting scarier by the second. I can feel my heart hammering in my chest, and I haven't even had to face Mom or Nana yet.

I hear Mom, Nana and Aunt Cayleen come into the courtroom behind me. It is just a feeling at first, but then I recognize a familiar voice. By the sounds of it, they are getting settled a few rows behind me, but in front of the pizza guy. Even though it is just a whisper, I recognize one of the voices immediately. It is Nana saying something about grandchildren. My heart sinks as I sit there thinking about what a disappointment I must be to her, my mom, and my whole family. *What? They hadn't been through enough? I had to add to the incredible heartbreak, disappointment, and embarrassment? It wasn't enough that Gramps had died last November, my dad shot to death about two weeks ago, and now I'm robbing pizza stores and hanging out with hoodlums! Real impressive stuff, Brooks. Who knew that name would be so*

notorious in such a short amount of time? The whole thing was
pathetic.

Suddenly the judge motions and the bailiff comes forward, "All rise." Everyone rises in the courtroom. I stand at the nudging of my attorney. The bailiff, standing at the front of the room booms out more instructions.

"Oyez, oyez, oyez… Juvenile Court for the county of Wayne, is now in session, with the honorable Judge Wilbert Cousins presiding. All present with business before this court be noticed, there will be no interruption in the courtroom. Any outbursts will be met with risk of immediate expulsion or possible contempt of court charges. All present may be seated," the bailiff concludes, and stands at attention to the side of the judge's bench.

"The Juvenile Court of Wayne County will now hear the case against Anthony Thomas Brooks. Council for the prosecution please read the charges," Judge Cousins directs. The lead county prosecutor read the charges.

"Council for the defense you may bring your case," the judge allows. At that, Mr. Arnett stood before the judge and went over the facts, as I had shared them and what had been reported to him by the police. He put forth all the reasons why the judge should be lenient with the sentencing, and the extenuating circumstances that surrounded my case and the fact that without the money bag, there was a lack of evidence in the case.

"Your Honor, Sir… if it would please the court, my client's mother wishes to speak on behalf of her son," my attorney implores.

The judge nods and replies, "I'll grant it."

I watch my mother approach the judge's huge, dark

mahogany bench. She looks so small standing there, dwarfed by the immense size of the wooden structure the judge sits behind. My heart aches for what I am putting her through. She glances at me on her way up to the front and the look on her face completely shatters my resolve to be just another no-luck, sad, lost, black kid from Detroit. My heart is pounding beneath my shirt, drumming in my ears, as my mother starts to speak with a trembling voice. I feel sick to my stomach. Jack Arnett walks from behind the table to go and stand beside Mom in front of Judge Wilbert Cousins, who was one scary guy.

"First, I'd very much like to apologize to the court on behalf of what my son did," Mom says very quietly. I look down at the floor. Right now, I could not look her in the eye, if I tried. I stand stiffly at my attorney's aide's side, behind the defense table, with my head down.

"Anthony's father was recently shot and killed on Anthony's fourteenth birthday," tears streak down my mother's face bringing black mascara along the telltale trails. "It's been hard---doubly hard, after..." Mom looks back at her mother dabbing the tears from her own eyes. "His grandfather passed less than a year ago," Mom is struggling to hold it together. I can hear the tears in her voice. I can see the strain this is causing her. "I know that my son is a good boy, Your Honor," her sniffles mix with her words. "He's never been in trouble before. He just got mixed up with the wrong crowd," there is quiet desperation in her voice, as she pleads to the judge for me. " I beg the court to have leniency on my son and give him a second chance," Mom's voice cracks and she puts her head down as she says barely above a whisper,

"Something my husband will never have," Mom breaks down into tears. Jack Arnett holds her up, leading her back to her seat. I keep my face pointed at the floor.

"Will the prosecution call your main witness?" came the judge's terse request.

"The prosecution calls Officer Bernard Scagliotti," calls out the lead prosecutor. Officer Bernie walks forward to the witness box, takes the oath to, 'Tell the truth, the whole truth and nothing but the truth.' He sits down and faces the courtroom. He never even looks my way. I'm grateful for that. The lead prosecutor begins,

"Officer Bernard Scagliotti, this is your name, correct?"

"Yes, sir it is," Bernie the Badge answers matter-of-factly. I am sure he has done this dozens of times.

The prosecutor continues, "And are you employed by the City of Detroit as a patrol officer in the area of Eight Mile Road and the westbound Ford Freeway?"

"I am," the cop answers again. *I never knew testifying in court was so proper, and totally boring! I thought everyone already knew all this.*

"And were you on duty the evening of August 27, 2009?" another question from the prosecutor.

"I was," Bernie the Badge answers quietly.

"And are you the brother of Joe Scagliotti, owner of Joe's Pizzeria, which is the establishment that was allegedly robbed on Saturday, August 27, 2009?" the prosecutor presses.

"That is correct," another clipped answer from Bernie.

"Could you tell the court your recollection as to the details of that evening, and how the defendant, Anthony

Thomas Brooks, was involved?" The prosecutor finishes, standing quietly by, waiting for the officer's response.

Bernie goes on to tell all the convicting details of what had transpired from the minute he had walked in the door of the pizzeria until the handcuffs were firmly snapped on my wrists. I had to admit he did an accurate job of relaying the story. He remembered some stuff I had forgotten about until he brought it up again on the stand. He told how, after I was cuffed and sitting on the ground, he had heard fleeing footsteps from behind him and turning quickly had seen someone running off clutching what looked like a bag, but he admitted that he had only seen the back of a dark, vest-style jacket and a pair of black tennis shoes. I felt my face flush at this revelation. His telling statement had confirmed that someone else had been there, too. Clearly, they didn't know it was TJ. I am sure that my attorney had not missed that tidbit of information, since he'd been looking at me with a riveting stare through most of the testimony the police officer was giving. Bernie the Badge finishes his stint in the witness box and returns to his seat after being dismissed by the prosecutor. Mr. Arnett's assistant has been madly taking notes throughout Bernie's testimony.

"Mr. Arnett, does the defense have anything further to add, before I make my ruling on this arraignment?" asks the judge dourly.

Mr. Arnett stands to face the judge. "Your Honor, if it please the court? I would like to remind the court of the fact that the stolen money has not been recovered, which would lead to the conclusion that others are also directly responsible in this crime. My client has no previous record of any wrong doing whatsoever. In addition, my young client has been experiencing a great deal of emotional strain due to the death of his father. Recently another witness with information about this case has come forward with incriminating evidence which involves multiple people in this crime," Mr. Arnett continues pleading my case with great conviction. He is suddenly interrupted by the judge.

"Why wasn't this witness, with additional information, called to testify, councilman?" inquires the judge.

"The witness is a minor, Your Honor. The court is protecting him from retaliation should his assistance in this case be revealed. I have additional information to share with you concerning this witness' testimony. He is listed on the witness list, and the prosecution did question him in a deposition early this morning," Jack finishes with command.

I didn't know exactly what my attorney was talking about with all those big words, but I was pretty sure I knew who the mystery witness was.

"Does the prosecution have any objection to this matter?" Judge Cousins pursues.

"We do not, Your Honor. The deposition will support our position," finishes the head of the prosecuting team. She is one smart cookie.

"In addition, if it please the court...," Mr. Jack Arnett carries on, "My client has assured me, that all truth and disclosure will be forthcoming regarding this misdemeanor. The defense is asking for your leniency in this case, as clearly some coercion has taken place in the commission of this crime, and no weapon was used.

Council will confer with Your Honor at the conclusion of this arraignment," Jack finishes and sits down quietly to await the judge's decision. It is absolutely silent in the courtroom. The judge sits quietly without speaking for some time, while everyone else does the same... waiting.

"Would defense council, the defendant, and Mrs. Brooks, mother of the defendant, approach the bench?" Judge Cousins requests. Mr. Arnett motions for me to go ahead. He waits for my mother to reach us, then stands between us, facing the bench.

The judge hesitates, clearing his voice. "Because this is an arraignment of a minor, I choose to speak to the parents or guardians in these matters. Mrs. Brooks, while I am truly sorry for the recent loss of your father and more currently the death of your husband, robbery remains a serious offense. I therefore, do not believe that ..." A huge lump starts to form in my throat. I know what is coming next. I can hear Mom's muffled sobs. I reach past Mr. Arnett to take my mother's hand. Suddenly there is a commotion from behind me.

A voice booms out, "Your Honor, please, a word."

The judge pounds his gavel and gruffly barks, "Order! Order in my court!"

The bailiff starts forward in the direction of the disruption. Mr. Arnett, Mom and I turn around at the same time to see what is happening. Joe Scagliotti, the pizzeria guy is standing up from his seat, holding out his hands to calm things down, "Your Honor, if it please the court, may I have a word with you?" Joe causes a ripple of surprise in the courtroom. Everyone is staring at Joe standing in the gallery. Nana and Aunt Cayleen are turning in their seats to see who is speaking. Judge Cousins motions Joe up to his bench, with the bailiff following close on his heels. Joe is limping very visibly through the courtroom and up to face the judge. The three of us move out of the way and allow him access to the aisle. Mr. Arnett and I walk back to stand by the defense table. Mom quickly returns to her seat.

"Approach the bench, Mr.?" the judge questions with authority.

"Scagliotti, sir. I'm the owner of Joe's Pizzeria; the store robbed by the defendant. I'm Joe Scagliotti, Your Honor. May I speak?"

"You do realize that you could be held in contempt of this court, Mr. Scagliotti?" Judge Cousins scolds.

"I do, Sir. However, before a breach of justice is done, I have to speak my piece," the pizza guy implores. "Please just hear me out," Joe, the Pizza guy, whispers only loud enough for the judge to hear him. The judge listens intently, and seems to be collecting his thoughts.

Suddenly, Judge Cousins slams his gavel on the bench and orders, "We'll take a short fifteen minute recess. Mr. Scagliotti, I'll see you in my chambers, along with both councils."

The judge motions for Joe to go ahead of him, and watches as he limps with effort, through the door behind the courtroom bench, followed by my attorney, his assistant, the prosecutor and her aide. The bailiff comes and stands beside me at the table. Everyone in the courtroom sits in stunned silence for several seconds, but the chatter soon begins in earnest. I can hear Nana's questioning voice, mumbling something to Mom and Aunt

Cayleen. Thankfully it sounds as if Mom has stopped crying. I hear her say clearly, "Bless that man to Heaven and back!"

Twenty minutes can seem like an hour. It sure did today. Finally the door behind the bench opens. The six people, who disappeared through it, now reappear intermittently and take their former places. Joe and the judge reappear last, several minutes after the others, and court resumes.

"All rise," the bailiff orders routinely. Everyone in the courtroom stands. "This court will now resume its session," the bailiff finishes and walks to stand next to the closed double doors.

The judge declares loudly as his gavel hits the platform on the desk's shiny, wooden surface, "Everyone may be seated. Both councils, will approach the bench."

My attorney, Mr. Jack Arnett, and the prosecuting attorney walk to stand in front of the judge. Honorable Judge Wilbert Cousins renders his verdict:

"First of all, let me address both councils on this matter. Had full disclosure been addressed in the notes for this arraignment, we may have avoided much of this altogether," comes the judge's sharp reprimand. "Since all appropriate steps in the pre-arraignment of a minor did not take place, and since substantial outside coercion appears to have occurred prior to the crime, and since the stolen money in question has not yet been recovered by police, and since this is a first offense for the defendant Anthony Thomas Brooks," the judge hesitates as if he is still thinking things through, "A sentence of required and continuous community service is rendered by this court upon the defendant, Anthony Thomas Brooks." The honorable Judge Wilbert Cousins continues:

"The following stipulations shall be followed to the letter of the law or risk of possible reversal of this rendered sentence to formal detention may be incurred. Mr. Scagliotti has generously allowed the defendant to work at his pizzeria, until which time the money taken has been paid back in full."

Someone in the courtroom draws in a shocked breath at the decision of the judge. I could hear people turning to look. I am imagining who that reaction had come from by the location of the sound in the courtroom, and the direction people had looked. *The expression on the pizzeria girl's face must be one of total disbelief!*

The judge bangs his gavel. "Order in this court, or you will be removed," Judge Cousins barks. No further reaction is heard. He waits for the courtroom to settle and proceeds with the sentencing.

"In exchange for a sentence of juvenile detention in an assigned facility, Anthony Thomas Brooks will complete required community service under the direction of Mr. Joseph Scagliotti, in order to pay back all monies, of which Mr. Scagliotti was unfairly deprived. The amount, determined to be $590.00 according to Mr. Scagliotti's financial records, is approved and certified by this court. Furthermore, the defendant and Mr. Scagliotti will meet with the court appointed caseworker on a weekly basis. The court officer will place in record for the court the amount of fine that has been accrued per week, and any work days missed. In addition, a stipulation is ordered by this court, that a minimum of $50.00 be accomplished weekly, and due to school responsibilities no more than 20 hours per week be required for work," commanded Judge Cousins with finality.

Addressing me directly and looking me squarely in the eye when I look up at the call of my name, the judge asks, "Anthony Thomas Brooks, is there anything you do not understand about what has just been said here or the judgment you are under from this court and the state of Michigan?" comes the judge's formal inquiry.

"No, Sir, I mean Your Honor, Sir…I understand," I stumble over my words. Someone could be heard stomping loudly out of the courtroom. *I bet I can guess who just made that exit*, I think to myself.

"Very well then… the defendant, Anthony Thomas Brooks is released into the custody of his mother, Mrs. Michele Brooks," the judge lifts up his gavel, hesitates for a second, as if wanting to say more, but then… Bang! "Court adjourned!" he loudly proclaims.

I can hear Mom crying. I'm sure her tears are from the shock of me not having to go to juvie. I can hardly believe what I had just heard. *What did that old man do that for? Now I was going to be beholding to some washed up pizza guy with a limp! I would have to go in every day to face those people, with them knowing what I did, and hating me for it!* I turn and stare at Joe, the pizza guy, letting all my pent up anger show on my face. I had to do it, but I didn't have to like it!

At least for Mom's sake I won't be in jail. Right now, jail seems preferable to having to do what that old guy tells me. *Forget working with this pizza girl, pretty or not, she will never get along with a guy who put their mitts in her Uncle*

Joe's till. It is for sure she isn't getting over somebody like me doing something like stealing from her family. I glance back at Mom, Nana, and Aunt Cayleen. They are all crying, but this time from relief.

CHAPTER NINE

or me life is about as dismal as it gets when you're fourteen, and this is my short list. It is Saturday, and my first day of going to the pizza place to work off my court ordered slave labor. I've been in a bad mood all week. After the court appearance Mom grounded me for a month. I am dreading the day I have to go back to school, and it is fast approaching. James and I can only talk on the phone once a day for no more than 15 minutes. I don't even need that long, 'cuz I'm not real talkative these days! In fact, don't care much for talking at all. It is awkward talking to people. Friends and neighbors all have that same look in their eye and tone to their voice of not knowing what to do or say. Everybody is treating me as if I will break, like a shattered egg, if they say the wrong thing.

Mom and I aren't talking much either, not for lack of her trying. She is so relieved to have me home and not in juvenile detention, that she has been leaving me alone with time to myself. We did have a conversation just this morning. I was down in the basement lifting weights, working off some tension. I was taking a break from my drawing. My basketball player sketches were all starting to look the same. I just couldn't seem to come up with any new action shots that were interestingly different, or that I liked.

Mom comes walking into the end part of the basement, carrying a laundry basket. I am sitting on the lifting bench just about to raise two ten pound hand weights above my head for my tenth rep.

"Just coming down to get the clothes out of your hamper," she offers as an excuse for being down here in my territory. "What time are you due at work today?"

"Mom, 4:00-8:00, same as every day that I will have to work there," I mutter.

"Anthony, I want you doing your best at Joe's place. It is a real blessing that Mr. Scagliotti has such a kind heart toward you and our situation. He didn't have to do that you know. If he hadn't, you would be living in a detention center, and not at home. You listen to my words, and be respectful to him, and do whatever he asks of you without complaint. I will be checking in with him to make sure you are minding and respecting him and this family! Nana will have nothing less and you know it to be true!" Mom finishes with as strong a voice as I have heard her use in a very long time. She can be tough! I know that. With my dad gone, she probably thinks she has to be, "You don't have to like it. You just have to do it right!"

"I hear you, Ma! I wouldn't call six months or more of slave labor a blessing, but whatever! I will do what that Scagliotti guy says I have to, but I won't be liking it, and no one can make me like it! I won't be doing anything else to cause you more pain. We've all had enough of that to last a lifetime! Don't worry. Nana will be satisfied!" I finish my words to her, feeling like I am a volcano about to blow! I'm strangling in the attempt to keep from shouting or crying or somehow expressing whatever is going on inside of me.

"I love you so much, Anthony. Your dad will be helping you get through this. He never would have wanted this for you. He loved you very much, don't forget that," Mom pleads reaching out to me. I move away from her touch. I want to punch-kick a hole in the wall.

"You can leave him out of this, thanks! I wouldn't be in this jam in the first place, if it weren't for him," I flash back angrily.

"Anthony, Anthony…" is her sad rebuke, but she says nothing more, just turns around holding the basket and walks down the hall shaking her head back and forth slowly. I stare at the wall, where a smaller picture of Mr. Big Shot hangs. He is taking a jump shot which has dead aim for the net. I kick the bench as hard as I can, then stand up to face the broken hockey game that I had kicked into oblivion. *What a dumb gift for a fourteen year old.*

Later, as I'm dressing for work, I run the scenario over and over in my mind about how my first day back to school will roll out. It is a day which is fast approaching. Going to work, for the first time, in a place where no one really knows me is one thing. Going back to school is something entirely different. Probably most of the kids at Warren Middle School already know I am a Juvie. I know the teachers do, because Mom and I had to go to the principal's office and sign up for counseling, also part of the court order for juvenile delinquents. *Wow! Don't ever do something this stupid again, Brooks! That's just plain ignorant. When this is over and you are done with Joe the Pizza Guy, keep your nose clean and don't ever, ever forget what a total pain all this was!*

I roll into work at five minutes to four. The sound of my skates on the tile floor is not easy to miss. I skate up to Joe Scagliotti standing behind the counter. He has on an apron that reads 'Joe's Pizzeria'. Joe's eyes drop to my rollerblades.

"My brother says you move pretty fast on those things," Joe comments.

"Obviously, not fast enough," I reply. Joe grins flashing his silver-capped tooth, getting my irony.

"You ready to get started?" Joe asks.

"Do I have a choice?" I ask in return.

"Not really," Joe states plainly, and hands me a broom.

"Now is as good a time as any, I guess," I retort.

"You wearin' those skates to work in?" Joe asks incredulously.

"I wear these like most people wear shoes. Whenever I'm not at home or in class, I have them on," I answer back in an even tone.

"Well, the first time you spill anything while you're wearin' those skates, or run over my toes or those of a customer…? You'll be wearin' your shoes or socks instead. You can start with sweeping the store. When the customers start coming in, I'll expect you to bus; that means clear off the dishes and trash from the tables, and wipe them clean with the disinfectant spray," I nod my understanding. "Sometimes I'll need you to help out in the kitchen."

I start looking around at the pictures hanging on the wall. Everything is about hockey. I see a picture of Joe wearing a Detroit Red Wings' uniform. I wonder what that's about. Mr. Scagliotti keeps on talking.

"Sonya, my niece, will show you where you can find all the cleaning supplies. You do what she tells you. She knows how to run this place almost as good as me," Joe finishes with a proud half smile.

"How long do I have to do this?" I ask with disinterest.

"Until you pay back what you owe me," Joe states simply. I look at him with a question in my head.

"How much do I owe you again?" I ask out loud. Joe starts digging in his pockets and pulls out a crumpled up piece of notebook paper, which he looks over very carefully.

"Six hundred dollars give or take a little. It'll still be just shy of me getting new uniforms, but it will help," Joe admits.

"Pizza uniforms?" I ask with confusion.

"Hockey uniforms," Joe answers and hands me a dustpan to go with the broom. "The clocks running. Start in the front room, and try to keep down the dust. Oh, and don't forget to take out the trash."

"Whatever you say, Boss!" I answer sarcastically. I skate away to start sweeping the front of the pizzeria. I can feel Joe's eyes boring a hole in my back. I already hate this job, and I haven't even been here ten minutes.

The whole week life seems about as bleak as it can get. Making matters worse, is the fact that school will be starting next week. Summer break is coming to an end and I dread facing school about as much as I do appearing in court. It will feel like being tried all over again, but every day, not just in a court of law. The kids at school will start acting weird and not know what to say about my dad getting himself killed while robbing a store. They will make a big deal about me getting arrested. It isn't as if things like this never happen in Detroit or other big cities. It is the fact that things like this never happen to me or my family.

Summer vacation always has to eventually come to an end. It is day one of being back at school. It hasn't been as bad as I thought it would be. Everyone is just leaving me alone, mostly. I can tell that a lot of the kids have heard the latest news about the Brooks' kid being a convict. Small groups of students standing around in the halls whisper when I walk past. Schoolmates, from former classes, look down at the floor when I approach. Only James comes up and talks to me like nothing is wrong. He meets me at my locker after the final bell sounds, and class is dismissed.

"Hey Anthony, glad to hear you didn't have to go to Juvie," James greets me quietly with a slight smile, and a pat on my back.

"You snitched on T.J. to my attorney, didn't you?" I whisper with exasperation. "Are you nuts? If T.J. or any of his gang ever find out, you're dead meat, and if I'm with you, so am I!" I was talking into my locker in hushed tones so no one else could hear.

"Well there's no way he's going to find out. Besides, nothin' happened to him, except he got a boatload of cash he's probably already spent on who knows what! Besides, wasn't letting my best friend go to Juvie, over something that creep put you up to in the first place! I told you I got your back, and I do!" James finishes through clenched teeth but also keeping his voice low and inaudible so that anyone passing by or standing near couldn't hear.

"Well, I might as well be in jail! I'm grounded for eternity. It's go to class. Come home. Change clothes. Go to work. Come home. Life is really a pain right now!" I complain bitterly.

"It won't last forever, man. It's a whole lot better than being in the joint! In a few more weeks we can be together and get over to the new outdoor skate park on Gratiot near Oakland. All the inliners who have been, say it's really awesome! We can work on speed and maneuvers on the new circular street course there," James finishes on a more positive note.

"Maybe, if I survive that long!" I whine.

"How long you gotta work at the pizzeria?" James pries.

"Until I pay back almost $600.00!"

"Ooh-Eee that's goin' to hurt! Hang in there, Shooter. I have every confidence in you! Gotta' go. Catch ya' later," James calls over his shoulder as he heads for the door. "Watching Jaden and Ameika today for my mom," and he is out the door and gone. At least this day at school was over.

Day two at the pizzeria, and one hour to quitting time. I am mopping the floor behind the counter and for me eight o'clock can't come too soon. I set the mop against the back door wall, and head for the front room to clear the dishes from the tables where customers had finished their pies and left. No one is in the pizzeria presently, so I am in no hurry. I pile the glasses, plates and silverware in one of the plastic tubs that Joe uses for bussing tables, and carry it to the kitchen.

Sonya glares at me as I come through the door, her usual greeting. I walk back to the sink. She continues what she is doing without so much as one word to me. Going into the kitchen is not my favorite thing to do. Sonya hangs in there a lot, and she is a force to be reckoned with! She hates my guts that is obvious. She has barely spoken to me since I started. Whenever she looks at me, which is almost never, she has a look on her face that is beyond contempt. She is never going to get past me stealing from her uncle, so I just try to stay out of her way. I'm paying for my sin, so I can do without her dagger looks and bristly ways. I put the dishes in the sink of sudsy water and walk out. I will wash them later, just before I leave. By then, hopefully she won't be in the kitchen.

The cowbell above the door clangs loudly. I look up and who comes walking through the door, but Mom and Nana. I scowl when I see the two of them. *What in the world are **they** doing here? Are you kidding me right now? This is really embarrassing! Mom, please! Checking up on me I suppose.* I offer a very weak smile.

Mom and Nana sit down at a booth that is set up like a penalty box. Both of them are smiling right at me. I skate over to see what they have to say. "Hi, Sweetie," Mom chirps.

"What are you doing here, Mom?" I press with exasperation and humiliation. An awkward moment follows.

"We are hungry, so we came here to eat," she answers innocently.

"Why can't you go somewhere else to eat, like Louie's Ribs?" I snap almost unable to control my frustration.

"My son doesn't work at Louie's Ribs," she states simply.

"This isn't work, it's illegal!" I immediately add. "I'm fourteen. Isn't child labor illegal?" I argue.

"Not if you're just doing dishes and wiping tables. Anyway, I gave the court my consent, so that makes it all square!" she counters.

"Thanks, Mom. It's nice to know you have my back," my sarcasm obvious.

"You're lucky to have your mother in your corner, Anthony. Don't you forget it! Besides, I wanted to come and see where you are hanging out so much…nice place!" Nana always looks for the positives in life, another of her qualities.

Sonya approaches the booth where Nana and Mom are sitting. Completely ignoring me, she whips out a notepad and pencil and asks in a friendly voice, "Ladies, what can I get you to drink?"

"Water, please," Mom responds looking over the menu.

"I'll have lemonade. Hard," Nana orders.

Mom shakes her head in disbelief, "Mother!"

"Oh, sorry, just make that a lemonade for me, no ice," Nana pipes up with a chuckle and smile.

It is obvious that Sonya has no idea the two women she is waiting on are related to me. Sonya actually smiles back at Mom and Nana, "I'll get those drinks right out to you."

On her way by Sonya turns to me. I'm holding the mop again, with my face as red as a beet; I am quite sure!

"There's a bucket of moldy onions that needs to be dumped out back," she forces a sarcastic smile through clenched teeth. "Could you see to that since you don't seem to be too busy right now?" Sonya walks quickly to the counter to fill the drink order.

"She's cute," Mom offers.

"You said the same thing about Gramp's Pit Bull," I counter.

"Didn't he bite you?" adds Nana.

"Twelve stitches," I remember with a shiver.

"Well, she seems all right to me! Testy... but cute," Nana ends. All I can do is roll my eyes and skate away. This is adding up to one crappy day.

Sonya brings the drinks to the table for Mom and Nana, "So, have you decided?" Sonya asks pleasantly as Mom is still perusing the menu.

"Let's see. What's your Power Play pizza like?" Mom points specifically to the item on the menu.

"It's what we call a full attack pizza. Has everything on it, or five listed items that you choose," Sonya informs, waiting patiently for the order.

"Can you make it without anchovies? I prefer my fish in the water, not on my pizza, thank you," Nana says with a wink.

"You got it," Sonya writes down the order on the tablet, and hurries away toward the kitchen.

Nana looks around at the framed pictures of the white hockey players hanging on the walls of the pizzeria. She is particularly eyeing the one closest to her, hanging just about eye level. "You hardly ever see any black hockey players. Why is that?" Cora Jones harrumphed with exaggeration to her daughter.

"Mom, when was the last time you were at a hockey game?" Michele affectionately snickers at her mother.

"Never," Nana answers with chagrin. Michele rolls her eyes at her mom for effect. Cora purses her lips with a wag to her head.

Suddenly a loud banging noise sounds from the back of the diner. The other customers also hearing the ruckus stop, in the midst of whatever they are doing, looking up immediately to see what is happening.

"Uhhh!" Nana gasps, clutching her chest as though she's having a heart attack. "A drive by?" she asks with alarm. Michele rolls her eyes with humor.

"Ma, we're at a pizza house, not a crack house," they both look toward the back of the restaurant to see Joe turning to look at Sonya who has just stuck her head through the order window to see what the commotion is about. Another round of banging follows. Bam! Bam! Bam! This time Joe comes from behind the counter, heading in the direction of the sound.

Other customers start standing with concern. "What is going on?" Joe demands as he limps toward the back door and disappears into the alley. Sonya follows quickly behind. She returns momentarily with a look of total disgust on her face. She starts assuring everyone that all is well. The customers start settling back into their unfinished meals.

"Just some wanna'be kid thinking he's a hockey star!"

93

Sonya snorts with disgust. Several customers chuckle. Michele looks at her mother with some concern.

Joe enters the alley quietly and cautiously, not sure of what to expect. He is surprised to see Anthony, with mop in hand, shooting rotten onions at a row of trash cans behind the store. Joe stands with arms crossed watching in silence. Mindless of the fact that he is being watched, Anthony forcefully shoots another onion at the trash can target. Bam! The shot is a high miss to the left.

"That's quite a shot you got there!" Joe quips.

I stop short of taking another swing at the sound of Joe's voice. *If I'm lucky, I might get fired momentarily for getting caught messin' around when I should have been working; Yep, here it comes...juvie home for the next six months.*

"Now, all you have to do is work on that pitiful aim!" Joe adds.

He limps over to one of the trash cans and kicks it over with his good leg so that the open end faces me. Next, he comes over a little bit too close for comfort... grabs the mop out of my hands, glances down at the onion, on the ground in front of him, and then at me. In a split second, Joe smacks that onion so hard it practically tears a hole in the trash can. He hands the mop back to me, and without a backward glance walks back into the pizzeria.

I keep staring at the trash can in disbelief. The onion is totally smashed sticking to the sides from impact. The juice from the rotten thing was dripping down the inside of the can. The force of his shot was amazing enough, but that onion had hit the can dead on, straight center bulls-eye! *Well, chalk that up for a goal! Probably just a lucky shot.*

Still recovering from my surprise at Joe's obvious skill

94

at shooting onions into a trash can, I re-enter the pizzeria. Mom and Nana are getting ready to leave. Mom is paying the check and Nana shares how she has left Sonya a generous tip. I get the feeling that Nana likes Sonya.

I'm so grateful that today is a Saturday. No school. Work later. So I get to sleep in late this morning. It had been a restless night. My dreams were rambling. They drifted from Joe making me do all his grunt work, to shooting hoops with my dad, to Sonya being nice to me, to T.J. and his gang cornering me in an alley with no way out! In one dream, Joe and I were playing hockey and he was beating me bad! It all added up to not much sleep. I walk into the kitchen still sleepy-headed from my night of tossing and turning. Mom and Nana are squaring away breakfast things in the kitchen.

"Hungry?" Mom asks as she pecks me on the cheek. "There's cold pizza in the 'frig," I sit down in the kitchen chair.

"Nana, Aunt Cayleen and I are going to visit your uncle," Mom says quietly. I immediately show my feelings about that with a sour face and set jaw.

"Why would you do that?" I question with a sharp edge to my voice. "Aunt Cayleen doesn't have a choice, she has to go see him. She's married to him. But, I can't see any reason why you'd go," I pushed.

"Because he's family, Anthony. We have to see him sometime," Mom explains with emphasis.

"Not my family," I protest.

"Now, now Anthony," Nana soothes. "We're going. You're welcome to come, if you want to. Your Uncle Alonzo would like to see you. It's been awhile," Nana reminds gently. I rise from the chair and walk over to the refrigerator opening the door to take out the pizza box.

"Yah, well it's goin' to be a while longer, a **l-o-n-g** while longer! I don't want to see him, and I'm not going," I snap.

"What are you doing today, since you don't have to go to the pizzeria until later?" Mom questions nervously, changing the subject.

"Hanging out with James. We might skate in the Foodland lot over by the old church," I finish matter-of-factly. "Some of the other guys say it has a great smooth surface for skating, since the parking area blacktop is so new. Or, we might skate over to Roosevelt Park, since it's free," I verbalize the options for her.

"We'll be home later. Remember to lock the door when you leave. Stay with James and don't be going off by yourself anywhere!" Mom states with finality as she walks over and hugs me, almost knocking the pizza box out of my hand. Nana settles for a kiss on the cheek, and they are out the door.

"See ya' later," I call after them, and sit down to eat a piece or two of cold pizza. I pull out the three pieces of pizza left in the box and put them on the plate that Nana had set on the table for me. I hear the car start and see Mom backing out of the drive. I can't help but also see the lettering on the cover of the pizza box that reads 'Joe's Pizzeria'. I take the box and slam dunk it into the open waste basket by the back door. I walk into the living room with my plate of pizza, turn on the cartoon channel, and chill out 'til it is time to meet James.

We had been street skating for hours. We tried out

empty parking lots behind businesses, five streets over from our neighborhood. Wherever we skate, we work on improving our basic skating skills; speed, agility, and maneuverability. The concrete jungle which surrounds us every day is a smorgasbord for skaters if the cops leave us alone. It has taken me at least ten or twelve tries around one cone track behind a local elementary school, before I can manage the turns and curves without bumping any cones along the course. I've been street skating for years and finally, my blading skills are getting there. I am flying high. I seldom fall anymore, and I skate circles around James who still struggles to keep up.

James is tired from all his trying. Skating is really more my thing than his, but because I am his choice as a best friend, he keeps at it without complaint. He really is a great dude to have for a friend.

"Man, I'm whipped. Let's just slow down and enjoy the ride," James pleads. I could see he really meant what he was saying.

"Oh come on, James. I still have to go to work for a few hours tonight! If I can do it, you can!" I challenge.

"By the way, how's the job?" he asks with interest.

"You mean the job I get paid for, but **never** see the money?" I scoff. James looks at me saying, "Come on, dude! What did you think it would be like?"

"Seriously, this is slavery!" I complain as I fly by James doing a 90 degree turn on my heels.

"Well, it sure beats goin' to juvie! I'd say working for no pay is a lot better than being locked up for six months!" he yells after me. I come shooting back up the street and steer my blades backward and forward in lazy circles around James. He just keeps blading straight ahead.

"Yah, yah if you say so, James," I respond with boredom looking his way. Suddenly, he has my full attention.

I notice that he is motioning inconspicuously, behind his one hand, with his index finger near his body, pointing to a car parked on the corner. All heads in the car are watching us, as I turn to look in that direction. T.J. with Davon riding shot gun and three other guys in the backseat, are all taking in the scene of us skating toward them down the street. Suddenly the car motor revs up. T.J. pops the clutch and they do a 360 turn in the intersection. Smoke pours from under the tires. The high pitched screeching of rubber on pavement from the spinning wheels can be heard throughout the neighborhood. The car speeds off down the street, leaving black tire streaks clearly on the roadway. James and I look at each other silently with eyes wide. We turn around immediately and head for home.

CHAPTER TEN

$\mathcal{J}$t is late Sunday morning, just after church is out. I have to start my shift at Joe's early today, because he has some big event going on later. I must admit I am still thinking about the encounter James and I had with T.J. and his gorilla guys the night before. I am sweeping the back storage room and absent-mindedly rewinding T.J.'s show of bravado, when he had spun a doughnut in the middle of the street. He was mocking my turns and circles which he had watched me do as James and I came down the street. *What a loser!*

Joe suddenly barges through the back door, startling me out of my reverie. He breezes by me without so much as a 'Hello', grabs some big visibly heavy cardboard boxes and two bags from the top shelf and motions for me to help manage the load. I grab the box closest to me and look at Joe questioningly.

"I need you to help me move some equipment," Joe blurts out gasping for breath.

"Pizza equipment?" I ask, puzzling about the timing.

"Hockey equipment," comes Joe's clipped response. I accidentally let slip a fake laugh, indicating my inward thought... *Like, this isn't my job.*

But I say, "What? You can't do it yourself ?"

"Not with this bum leg," he points out with frustration.

My eyes drop down to his bad leg. "That's what I got you for," he grins.

"What happened?" I ask not really sure I even care.

"Got my knee blown out," his answer surprises me.

"Gun shot?" Joe chuckles at my question.

"Slap shot," he finishes and walks out the back door with me following behind.

After loading the bags and boxes into Joe's battered van, we head to 'I don't know where'. We drive across town to a place on the southwest side and pull in to Scagliotti's Ice Arena. Joe drives up to a big ramp area in the back and parks the van. We get out of the truck without a word. I look up at another big sign hanging above a huge double door entrance in the back. It reads: **Scagliotti's Ice Arena**, with **Home of the Ice Dragons** printed in block letters beneath.

"You own a skating rink, too?" I ask with surprise. Joe just nods without looking at me. He's all occupied with getting the boxes out of the back of the van. "It looks like the car plant where my dad used to work," I say out loud with memories flashing in my head of yearly summer picnics when all the guys who worked on the line came with their wives and kids.

Joe keeps to the task at hand saying, "It's actually divided into two arenas. One side for hockey and the other for figure skating," Joe explains.

"You ever play hockey?" I ask with increased interest, as we start pulling bags and boxes of hockey equipment out of the back of the van. "Probably not, hockey is for white guys," I add as I yank a bag from under a box. Joe stops and raises an eyebrow at me. We both look at each other.

"Uh huh, really?" Joe hesitates a moment then adds, "Tell that to Val James, the first African American to play in the NHL, and Brian Johnson, or Nathan Robinson, who both played for the Detroit Red Wings. A lot more, too," another pause from Joe, then "Besides, the only color hockey fans see on the ice is red; blood-red. I look at Joe with wide-eyes and then notice the Red Wing bag he is holding.

"So, you played," I state warily, not really believing he would say yes, and not knowing if I should believe him if he did say 'yes'.

"Ah, little bit. Previous lifetime," comes his clipped reply.

"How many years?" my interest is definitely coming alive as Joe ponders my question.

"Twenty-seven," he continues calculating in his head.

"Twenty-seven years?!" I repeat his statement with amazement.

"I started when I was five. Quit when I was thirty-two," he finishes.

"Wow! Why did you quit?" now I couldn't stop asking the questions. Joe makes a goofy grin, playfully sharing his answer, "Got my bell rung one too many times. Besides, it was time to hang up the blades. Thirty-two-year-old legs aren't the same as twenty-two year old legs," he nods his head in affirmation of his statement.

"I saw you wearing a Red Wing's jersey in your pizzeria," I state simply. Joe's eyes come back to mine before he answers seriously.

"Yep. Played a season for the Wings," he admits.

"Only a season?" I really want to know the answer to this one.

"We were playing the Flyers. One of 'em wanted to teach the new Red Wing a lesson he wouldn't forget," Joe sets the equipment bag down on the ground. "Bam! He crushed my knee and my professional hockey days were over," Joe shut the doors of the van with a hard thump. Picks up the bag on the ground, and heads for the back door of the ice arena. I grab a box and a bag and hurry after Joe.

Joe enters through the back door, opening it with a key he pulls from his pocket. I can hear the sound of voices and skates on ice followed by a Slap! The sound of a hockey stick hitting the puck or the wall or both. As our eyes adjust to the darkness of the arena passageway through which we are walking, I see the rink and the Plexiglas safety barriers surrounding it at both ends. A team is on the ice in full hockey gear from the helmets down to the pads on the knees and the skates. A guy wearing an Assistant Coach sweatshirt whistles a junior team through their drills on the ice. My steps start to slow as I watch with intrigue the whistle commands understood by the players. The sound of the whistle pushes them into the up and down laps they execute using precision footwork. The players' handling of the hockey sticks, when it came to taking their shots at the puck, is fascinating. I'm not even aware that in my interest for what is evolving on the ice, I have stopped. Joe continues walking on down the passageway. When he hollers at a far distance for me to catch up, I am blown away by the fact that I hadn't even realized that I had stopped walking. *Wow! What is this sport about?*

I hurry to catch up, keeping my eye on the action taking place out on the ice. *Some of those guys skate as well as me.* I watch with curiosity as the puck is maneuvered down the ice. The center player stops the puck on the blue line, aims and shoots, Bam! The puck zips into the empty net, as the center player goes down, decked from the side defender. The coach with the whistle clenched between his teeth, blows the whistle long and hard, ending the practice as he turns around to skate off the ice. Instant recognition… *Oh great! If it isn't Bernie the Badge, Joe's brother and the arresting officer, who testified against me in court. Wish I was anywhere but here right now.*

I stare nervously out over the ice and connect eye to eye with Bernie. He turns away to wave at Joe. The center skates over to a guy, with jet black hair, on crutches standing behind the wall watching the practice. He hands a water bottle to the center as the hockey player pulls off the helmet. A long dark ponytail falls from beneath the helmet. My eyes almost pop out of my head…the player under all that uniform and helmet is Sonya! *A real family affair I see!! I'm outta' here!*

I crouch down and head for the bleachers farthest away. In this spot, it's darker and harder to be seen beyond the bright lights out over the ice. I keep my back to the ice as I slink away, hoping I'm not noticed. Joe and Bernie are busy talking, so I know that Joe won't be needing me for a while. I climb up about four rows to sit down behind a pole. *More cover.* I glance over to see if Sonya has seen me. My heart sinks as she is looking in my direction, and the guy beside her is following her eyes to where she is looking. *Busted!* They must have been watching me make my escape the whole time. *Now that's embarrassing.* Sonya looks away with disgust.

I sit there sullenly watching as the team goes back out on the ice. Joe stays in the box, watching every move and calling out to this player or that one about their play. I stay where I am. He stays where he is, until the scrimmage is over. The team comes off the ice. The team and the other assistant coaches, including Bernie, gather around Joe for a post-practice session. There is a blanket of silence as everyone listens for Joe's words. He looks around the circle at all of his players.

"You've got to be tough out there, Dragons. Make good passes. Stop offensive rushes from happening. Most important, you got to be smart!" The team focuses on every word Joe is saying, "Especially, if we are going to reach our goal of making it deep into the playoffs." At Joe's words, the team looks around the tight circle at each other. "You got that?" Joe finishes with a loud question voiced for all standing there. The players and assistant coaches all nod.

"Yes, Coach!" the voices around the circle shout in unison. Joe shoots his hand out waist high. The team reaches out their arms, placing their hands on top of Joe's like a tall stack of pancakes.

"On three, ready...one...two...three," Joe counts loudly.

"Go Dragons!" the entire team shouts together, as they all lift their arms toward the rafters. The players leave the huddle and drift away to the locker rooms, talking with each other on the way.

Joe walks up the nearest isle toward me, but is struggling some with the steps and his bad leg. When he reaches my row, he walks over to where I am sitting and plunks himself down beside me. Before he arrived, I had picked up an old discarded program I spotted laying on the floor under one of the seats. I had been passing the time; drawing with the pencil, I always carry around in my pocket for sketching whenever I have a minute to spare. The main outline of the drawing was almost done, but I hadn't gotten all the details shaded in, since my interest at the activity happening down on the ice, kept me glancing away from my sketches.

Joe stares down at the drawing before him. It is clearly Sonya on the ice hurling a hockey puck into the goalie net. "Not bad," Joe sighs, venting his effort from climbing the steps. He glances at the other renditions of hockey equipment I have drawn around the edge of the sheet of paper. He shakes his head up and down and seems impressed.

"You think you can sketch a dragon?" he asks breathlessly. We both look at each other. "Seriously, we're going to need a drawing for our team's logo, some kind of dragon. You think you can do that?"

I laugh out loud at this inside joke, but am not getting sucked into this little family affair. "I draw what I choose to draw. Dragons aren't one of my choices. All I want to do is pay off what I owe you, and I'm out of here! Got that?" I reply for emphasis.

Then, as if he hadn't even heard what I just said,

Joe went on saying out loud what was obviously running through his head, "I'll tell ya' what I'll do. You do the sketch and I'll knock off a hundred bucks of what you owe me," his words instantly have my total attention. I sit up abruptly and look squarely at Joe.

"You're kidding, right?" I ask with excited disbelief.

Joe shakes his head, "Nope, not kidding." Joe pauses and then explains, "I want it to go on their new jerseys, but it's got to be good enough for the championship." Joe pauses again, "That is if we can make the championships without Vinnie on the ice," he finishes with concern.

"Who's Vinnie?" I ask distractedly, since I want to get back to the idea of working off a hundred dollars of what I owe in the easiest way possible for me. Joe glances down at the bench, and motions his head in that direction.

"Sonya's brother, the kid on crutches with the dark hair, my nephew."

"Brother?" I mutter with surprise. Joe looks at me and nods.

"Well, you think you can do it, draw a dragon I mean?" Joe presses the issue. I quietly consider the question, like I need more time to think about it or something.

"Umm, yah. I'll do it. I'll do anything that will get me out of your sweatshop." I don't want to seem too anxious, but I want the offer to stay on the table.

"Good," Joe reaches his hand out to shake on the deal, and shoots me a glance. "Oh, and the dragon needs to look bloodthirsty," he smiles.

"Yah, bloodthirsty," I look at him like he's crazy.

"This is a brutal sport, kid!" he gestures to his silver

tooth and broken nose. "You'd know that, if you ever saw Captain Crunch play," Joe puffs out his chest for effect.

"The dude on the cereal box?" I quip.

Joe cracks a smile, "No, Wendell L. Clark the dude who crunches players on the ice.

CHAPTER ELEVEN

I've been drawing all morning. There are pictures of dragons taped all over the wall above my desk where I have been working. The drawings are in black chalk and I have them hanging all around my poster of Chauncey, Mr. Big Shot, Billups. I am sitting in my chair looking carefully at each one with a critical eye. There is a knock on my door.

"Yup," I respond.

"Hi," Mom greets me as she opens the door and strolls over to my desk where I am still sitting and staring at the wall of drawings. "What are you doing?"

"Nothing," I reply looking down at my sketchpad.

"Looks like something to me," she counters.

"Just a sketch," I continue drawing.

"When did you get home?" Mom inquires.

"A while ago," I try to focus on my drawing.

"Is everything all right?" she continues the interrogation. I don't answer. "What are you drawing?" she pries, looking down more closely at what I'm sketching on my pad. I'm getting frustrated with trying to get the drawing right and no time for small talk.

"Mom, look at it… dragons," I answer shortly. Mom looks at the picture then raises her eyes to sweep across the drawings taped up around Mr. Big Shot.

"This isn't some kind of gang symbol is it?" she asks with a worried tone.

"No!" I reply with insult and injury in my voice.

"You remember what your father would tell ya'…you hang out with bad people, you become a bad person," she stresses.

"Maybe he should have listened to his own advice!" I snap back, looking her square in the eyes. Her eyes were welling up with tears.

"Mom, it's for Joe's hockey team," I say soothingly and walk up to hug her. She looks at me quizzically.

"Pizza Joe? Isn't he a bit old for playing hockey?"

"He's a coach, Ma," I answer.

"Of a hockey team?" she asks with surprise, trying to put this unexpected picture together.

"It's a junior hockey team for kids my age," I try to explain, as I sit back down on my chair.

"He's going to knock off a hundred bucks of what I owe him if I draw them a mascot, a dragon." I pick up my pencil. Mom looks down at what I'm drawing.

My dragon has a serpentine body with a twisting tail. It has horns along the back of the head and neck with clawed feet, and bat-like wings. Its nostrils flare with wisps of smoke coming out of its nose. Orange and red flames shoot out of its fire-breathing mouth. The dragon has emerald green eyes, and fanged teeth. The best part is the broken hockey stick clenched in its sharp, pointy teeth.

"Cool dragon! It looks like an ice sculpture," Mom observes.

"It's an Ice Dragon," I announce.

Mom nods, "Interesting."

"It's goin' to be the team's logo, that is if Joe likes it," I exaggerate with sarcasm. "Still have some details to finish before I let him see it."

Mom walks toward the door of my room then turns, "Oh! I almost forgot. Nana has packed some boxes. When you're done with your sketch could you please bring them down here and put 'em in the corner of the backroom?"

"Sure thing," I offer. She walks out closing the door quietly.

I stay at my desk for another hour of drawing. I'm beginning to feel frustrated, 'cuz I'm having no luck at getting the dragon to look exactly the way I want. Prompted by hunger pangs stabbing my gut, I decide to walk upstairs for a sandwich. I pass the boxes Nana has packed and stacked at the top of the stairs. I decide that now is as good a time as any to carry the boxes down to the basement and get that job done, but… after I eat.

The sandwich I fixed had satisfied my hunger and I was struggling now to carry one of the heavier boxes to the basement. I pass the table hockey game I got for my birthday, still laying on its dented side in disarray on the floor, and catch my toe just enough to jerk me hard but not make me fall. The flimsy box collapses and a slew of picture albums and framed photos tumble out onto the floor. "Arrghh! This is a bunch of junk!!" I shout and look around to see if anyone is coming down the stairs, or happens to be in earshot of my angry outburst. All silence.

I start picking up the stuff that had fallen to the floor, throwing it back in the box. It was an accumulation of years of memories. I paw through the jumbled pile spying an old cigar box. I open it and finger through a collection of saved trinkets: a pair of old cufflinks, a gold cross engraved on the back with the initials TAB. *Could that be my dad's? Thomas Anthony Brooks, initials TAB, had to be.* I sit down on the floor with the box between my legs. I continue exploring: A gold wedding band, a key to something, a silver dollar taped to the photo of a newborn baby. *This has to be me, boy was I ugly! I wonder why the picture is taped to a silver dollar.* I keep looking: the strap to a football helmet, a school class ring, a high school senior picture of an older version of me. Stamped in the corner in gold, it reads, Thomas A. Brooks-Class of '90. I hear the front door open and voices coming from the entryway. I shove the picture of my dad into my jacket pocket and finish throwing everything else into the collapsed box. I drag it over to the far corner of the backroom as James sticks his head around the stairway wall.

"You down here?" James' voice booms as he leaves the stairway and walks toward where I'm standing in the doorway of the backroom.

"Yah, right here," I say, making sure the picture is securely in my pocket.

"What's up, Shooter?" James uses his familiar cheery greeting.

"Moving boxes," I say with boredom.

"What's that?" James asks as he stares at the ramshackle, dented up hockey game table laying on the floor just inside the door of the backroom.

"My lousy birthday present," I reply with disdain.

"Don't look lousy to me. Let's play!" He shrugs. I look at him, stunned at his reaction.

"Look at it! It's a piece of junk!" I glare at him with anger.

James brushes off my angry reply. "I'm pretty good at fixing things, you know that. Let's see what we can do. Got some duct tape?" he smiles.

James has been known to work miracles with duct tape. This turns out to be one of those moments! Before long we're playing table hockey like it's a serious, real, live game of hockey going on right in my very own basement. James is on one end of the game table and I'm on the other. The table is a model of a real hockey rink in miniature, with nets at each end and cut-out characters for hockey players; all with white faces. The hockey puck is black, and the size of a very small, round clock battery. Two teams are represented, with players attached to long sticks that run through slots in the table "ice arena" floor. Six players on each side; one center, two forwards, two defense men, and a goalie. All are controlled by sliding the handles on the outside of the table back and forth to make the players move. The players' uniforms are two different colors, so each team is easy to sort out. I pick the team in the black and white jerseys. I let James be the red and white Detroit Red Wings team. *I want nothing whatsoever to do with that business! I'm sure not picking anything related to the Scagliotti bunch.*

James has the miniature puck in his end. He mimics a buzzer sound with his mouth, and we're off! We frantically spin and slide the players along the narrow slots trying to get control of the puck. James' center gets the puck. He rotates and shoots the puck. Slam! Into the opposing net it goes, and his team scores.

James jumps up and cheers loudly. "Yes! Make that One for my team!"

Now it's back to center ice, all the team players are in place as we position them with the controls, where we choose them to be. This time I make the buzzer sound and we're off again! My center hugs the puck. He passes it to the right forward. No shot. James is blocking with his defense. My right forward slides the puck back out to the center, which sends it flying to the left forward. Slam! Dead center into the net flying in from the left side; Score!

"Y-yes!" I smile. "Make that a tie game!" I crow.

"Anthony, dinner's ready!" Nana's voice calls from the top of the stairs. James wipes his brow in relief. We're both sweating by now.

"Tomorrow then? This is fun! I'll get you good. Wait 'n see!" James smiles. We both laugh. "Sweet birthday present!" James remarks with enthusiasm as he heads off up the stairs, "Later!"

The next day at school, the final bell of the school day sounds at last. Some days seem like they are never ending when it comes to school. I grab my backpack out of my locker and head for James' locker area. He is shoving his books onto the top shelf of his locker and pulling his backpack out, getting ready for the skate home.

"Yo, Shooter!" he smiles as I stop to stand next to his locker. "Let's put on our wheels and blow this dungeon!" he jokes. He smiles again. I don't. We both head for the main front doors.

"Glad to be done with this place for a few hours," I complain as we walk out the huge, heavy doors leading to freedom.

We sit down on the curb, which borders the student pickup area, out of the way of the traffic. We begin pulling out our skates and putting them on for the ride over to my house. We are having fun trash talking to each other about tonight's tie breaker game of table hockey. We can't wait to finish what we had started the night before. Suddenly, my cell phone rings. The caller ID pops up. I see it's from the pizzeria. I answer my cell, even though I don't want to hear what the caller has to say.

"What's up?" I ask with irritation in my voice.

Joe's voice is on the other end. "I need you to come to work this afternoon. As soon as you can get here," Joe insists.

I roll my eyes at James, "Yah, well I got plans. Besides I wasn't scheduled for work today," I argue.

"Yah, well change your plans. I need your help," Joe demands. I snap my phone shut, fuming. James knows I am ready to blow my cool. I explain with fury the annoying situation.

"Later, Shooter. We'll play tomorrow," and James was off.

CHAPTER TWELVE

When I arrive, I see Joe and Bernie through the window sitting at a booth opposite the front door of the pizzeria bent over something in concentration. As I push the door handle, the cowbell rings above the door. They both look up as I roll in the shop on my wheels. I skate over to where they are sitting, feeling nervous.

"So what's so important?" I inquire with tension in my voice.

"You're late, Brooks!" Joe snaps.

"Well, you're lucky I'm here at all, I wasn't scheduled to work today." I jerk off my backpack, without reacting to his obvious irritation because I am late, and pull out the sketch of my dragon. "Hey, Mr. Scagliotti," I stare at Joe waiting for a reaction. "I finished my drawing," I announce as I hand it over for Joe to have a look.

"What's that?" Bernie questions.

Joe examines the drawing closely. Instantly a huge smile covers his face.

"Our **new** team logo," Joe answers with conviction, as he passes the sketch to his brother. Bernie looks at the drawing, with no response.

"It's… an Ice Dragon," I explain. "Thought as long

as I had to come in today, I might as well bring it," I ease off on my anger over having to come in to work.

"Ice Dragon?" Bernie asks, somewhat puzzled by my explanation.

"The Ice Dragons," Joe nods. "Hmm... I like it!" he beams. I actually smile for once at something Joe has to say.

"Well, I'll give you this, kid. You got skills for drawing, that's for sure!" Bernie finishes with surprise, beaming a smile, too.

Joe fishes around in his pocket and pulls out a wadded up, dog-eared piece of paper. *Oh, yah...here it comes- the famous IOU note.* He picks up the pencil lying on the table and licks the tip before crossing out a number at the top.

"Lemme see...four hundred seventy-five minus one hundred. Now you owe me just three hundred seventy-five dollari..," Joe says with delight as I am listening to his last words in complete puzzlement. "Dollari, you know... dollars!" Joe finishes with a huge grin.

"I take that to mean, four hundred smackers. It might as well be a thousand!" I complain aloud. Joe smiles again, too wide for me to appreciate. Despite his gruff manner, I feel like Joe is actually enjoying my enslavement, and the discomfort it causes me. I skate off toward the back of the pizza parlor. I can hear Bernie and Joe snickering as I make my escape.

Sonya is kneading pizza dough as I come sliding into the kitchen. She immediately looks up at me and barks, "You're **late**!"

"I'm here! Be grateful I came at all! I wasn't even scheduled today!" I glare back at her and continue in words as biting as hers, "Yep, I'm late. So I've heard, twice now!" I grab the broom from behind the door and exit with my inlines clattering along the tile floor. *That girl gets on my last nerve!*

I bus the vacated tables and am busy throughout the dinner hour. No time for conversation or standing around. The dinner shifts are always like that. Now the dinner rush was waning, and not many people remained in the pizzeria shop. I was sweeping the floor minding my own business. Joe and Bernie were again seated at the same booth, both looking gloomy, like they'd lost their last friend or something. I couldn't help overhearing their conversation.

"It's going to be a struggle getting deep into the playoffs without Vinnie on the team," Bernie laments as he looks down at the team roster. "It'll be like the opposing teams having a power play against us every time we hit the ice," he continues to complain.

I am hearing and seeing more than I want to or should be, but I can't stop myself from listening. I continue my charade of sweeping the floor.

"It is times like this I wish Sonya was a boy," Joe added quietly. Bernie leans back looking at his brother with a perplexed expression.

"She's too much of a tomboy already. Her mother would roll over in her grave if she knew I was even allowing her to play hockey in a girls' league, let alone practicing with a boys' hockey team!" Bernie rakes his fingers through his head full of dark hair in exasperation. "It was Maria's dream for her to wear figure skates, not hockey skates," Joe pauses in thought at Bernie's comments.

Sonya comes walking out of the kitchen carrying a basin full of disinfectant cleaner. She starts wiping down the front counter with sudsy water. She never looks my way. She just keeps cleaning.

"What we need is someone who can match Vinnie's skills in skating, and has a commanding shot to go with it!" Joe points out the obvious.

Without a second thought, and completely on impulse, I skate over to the table and looking at Bernie and Joe, blurt out, "I'll do it."

Both men look up from their involved conversation, "Uh...you'll do what?" Joe asks slowly in confusion, my meaning not registering with either of them. They were oblivious to the fact that I had been sweeping nearby, eavesdropping the whole time.

"I'll fill in for Vinnie. That is, **if** you'll knock off another two hundred dollari," I dicker, mimicking Joe's earlier use of 'dollari' for dollars. Joe looks at me with astonishment.

"You're not kidding are you?" Joe responds in surprise. "But, it's not as simple as all that."

"Yah, inline skating and ice skating are two different things, kid," Bernie adds.

"What's the difference?" I hold my ground.

"Uh... BIG difference," Bernie says with emphasis. "Besides knowing how to skate, we need a point man."

I shake my head trying to understand, "A point man?"

"A center... a shooter," Joe explains patiently.

I lower my head, my voice, and narrow my eyes stealthily as I say, "You mean like a hit man?" I say in a teasing manner.

Both men laugh out loud. Joe shoots me a toothy silver-capped smile.

"Yah, like a hit man, but instead of shooting bullets, he's shooting pucks!" Joe and Bernie both laugh again, but harder this time.

Sonya is now at full attention, looking straight at me, with both hands still in the soapy water, and a fierce frown on her face. She had been eavesdropping, too.

And So It Begins...

As agreed, I head right over to the pizzeria after school is out on Monday. Joe has to be my ride, since Mom is still working. Joe and I ride mostly in silence over to the arena. We are both short on words. We lock the truck and walk, with duffle bags in hand, to the back entrance of the skating arena. Joe unlocks the door with his key.

Joe laces up and is out on the ice before I barely straighten out the laces on the pair of skates he has handed to me for practice. Joe had come up with them for my use, 'til he figures out if this is going to work out; that is, me playing for the Detroit Dragons. I stop in the middle of my lacing and watch in amazement as Joe shoots puck after puck directly into the net from any angle he chooses. *Man this guy's got a shot! He must have been really good!* I finish lacing up with similar thoughts swimming inside my head.

By the time I struggle out onto the ice Joe, Bernie, Vinnie and Sonya are all standing behind the boards watching me clumsily attempt the transition from wheels to blades. I am feeling like an idiot dressed in Vinnie's hockey gear, wearing who knows whose skates, with a helmet that is sitting on my pea-sized head like an oversized bucket! In addition to that, I can barely stand, let alone skate! Oh yes, they were all going to be entertained by this circus show! *Come on, how hard could this be? Concentrate on your balance: Just like skating on my inlines.*

As my mind continues running over the pounding instructions rolling inside my head, I can't help but notice the little family meeting going on behind the boards between Joe, Bernie, Vinnie, and Sonya. I am too far away to hear any of the heated conversation going on between them, but occasional arm raising, eye rolling, and general body language is telling me everything I need to know. I can only imagine what they are saying about me as a skater and their future hockey jock. I'm thinking, *Not too obvious who your topic of conversation is...* as they all stare without pretense at me trying to stay upright on the ice!

From the Bench...

"Well, at least Vinnie's skates fit him," Joe offers enthusiastically.

"Only after I stuffed in a couple of socks as fillers," Bernie counters.

Vinnie's eyes narrow as he offers begrudgingly, "I don't like other players using my gear, especially my skates!"

"Every once-in-a-while, you have to take one for the team," Joe lectures.

"Yah, well I can play better on crutches than he can on skates! If he's going to play at all, it should be in the Squirt Division! Where's all this great skating ability I hear this guy is supposed to own?" Vinnie objects. All eyes watch the ice as Anthony struggles to maintain his balance and stay on his feet.

"He is small," Bernie observes.

It is easy to see that Vinnie's uniform is about two sizes too big for Anthony. He keeps pushing up the sleeves, and the shirt tail hangs almost to his knees.

"You know, when you're small it makes you more aggressive," Joe follows up with conviction and a positive tone.

"Yah, you should know," came Bernie's little brother tease.

While Sonya's uncle, father and brother continue the debate about Anthony, Sonya is struggling with conflicting emotions of her own, as she watches Anthony spin around and fall on the ice. She is not letting go of her anger and blame toward Anthony for robbing her Uncle Joe, and she continues making that clear to everyone, including Anthony. Yet, she never dreamed it would be this hard watching Anthony's struggles and obvious embarrassment. Others stand snickering while witnessing his humiliation at being a true rookie in front of more seasoned players. Sonya feels that he deserves just what he's getting. She visibly cringes at some of his more degrading episodes on the ice. Though she doesn't want to admit it, Sonya recognizes that Anthony is trying hard to get things right, and it is not going his way. Sonya continues watching, steeling herself against any softening toward him. She isn't letting Anthony Brooks off the hook!

"This isn't a very good idea. In fact, it is a terrible idea!" Sonya flinches, as she realizes she had spoken aloud the thoughts running in her head.

"What? Why not?" comes her Uncle Joe's immediate resistance.

"Because…he's an inline skater, not a hockey player. Look at him! He can't even stand on ice skates, let alone use a hockey stick!" Sonya shoots back.

"He'll learn. It just might take some time," Joe argues.

"But in time for the playoffs?" Sonya persists with exasperation, despite her uncle's knitted brows and expression of determination.

"Joe, we have a whole team to be concerned about, not just one kid," Bernie comes to his daughters defense.

"We'll get him some one-on-one training," Joe refuses to give in, as Sonya shakes her head, rolling her eyes.

"And who's going to waste their time teaching **him**?" she persists, with an obvious point of her finger in Anthony's direction on the ice. At that comment, Joe, Bernie, and Vinnie turn their attention on Sonya's pointing finger as in unison they stare at Anthony trying to balance himself on Vinnie's skates. Sonya turns at the silence following her comment to find them all now staring directly at her.

"No! No way!!" she stammers and repeats with useless emphasis.

"'Every once-in-a-while you got to take one for the team'," Vinnie mimics his uncle's words and grins with satisfied retaliation. Sonya swats Vinnie soundly on the arm. She gazes out onto the ice and marvels at the task that lays ahead of her and Anthony. She knows there is no getting out of this one.

CHAPTER THIRTEEN

I turn my attention away from the Scagliotti family meeting and on to what really matters. I am more determined than ever that I will not play the fool for anybody. I will learn to master this ice skating if it takes all night! I work for over an hour just getting my legs used to the noticeable difference in the feel of the skates on ice rather than concrete. It is a thin line of balance on the blades rather than the wider wheels of inline skates. I grew-up learning how to maneuver on very different surfaces. There is some grip to sidewalks and streets, but this skating on ice is a whole new deal. I feel like I am floating, and sometimes flying across space with little or no control whatsoever. No bumps, or coarse, grainy surfaces to slow you down, or grab onto with some foot pressure on the wheels. Ice skating is a new game.

Moving across the ice feels as smooth as running your hand over a clean table top, like the feel of touching a well-worn leather jacket; sleek and slippery. With my inline skates, I can go up on my toes or lean on my wheels to control speed and direction. My body responds automatically to the sway and lean of the inline skates under my feet. I know those routines almost instinctively. This ice skating is a whole different feel! Straight blades with almost no give or bend: Full speed, straight ahead.

Turns are wider, and harder to maneuver in tight spaces. Just since hitting the ice, I've fallen at least a dozen times, but gradually I'm beginning to feel some degree of control return to my feet. My body is sensing a new center above the skates. I hope this adventure will be like riding a bike; once you learn how to do it, you never forget. I sure don't want to go through this humiliation again!

It had been a trying week since my first time on the ice and the public embarrassment I had endured. Two nights this week, Mom had driven me across town to the arena for more practice without an audience. I worked to improve my balance, control and speed. It has helped, but I'm still not where I want to be. I am glad that it is Saturday. No school, and no work at the pizzeria. Mom dropped me off at the ice arena an hour ago. My mind is in constant motion as I take the ice on my borrowed skates for a Scagliotti ordered pre-practice before my first team scrimmage. I am beginning to get the feel for this ice skating. No falls in at least the last ten minutes. I am trying wide turns and skating at faster speeds. I am still unsteady in sudden moves. *Man, this is challenging, and I haven't even had a hockey stick in my hand yet! Joe must be nuts to believe I can ever be ready to play in a hockey tournament that is only a few weeks away! I will prove Vinnie and Sonya wrong, about me being a loser at playing hockey! I will learn how to do this, and do it as well as my inline skating!*

I'm used to skating in shorts and a tee-shirt. All this gear is heavy! The sooner I learn to skate and shoot with all this equipment on, while opposing players defend my every move, the better I will get through the tournament. Then I can pay off my debt to Joe and earn my freedom from all this slave labor! It is going to be a **long** couple of months ahead.

Sonya suddenly comes skating over to me, as I just complete one full, fast skate around the rink along the boards. I am standing on the far side of the arena, adjusting Vinnie's helmet to my head. There is no hint of a smile or welcome on her face, as she sprays flying ice crystals all over the front of my shirt and pants, coming to a halt directly in front of me.

"Going onto the ice without the proper equipment is like a gladiator going into battle without his shield," she lectures as her hands clutch the hockey stick, which she holds in front of her and leans on like a post. I hate to admit it, but Sonya looks right at home wearing equipment which actually fits her body proportions. She looks poised and confident in her skills as a skater, and her place on the ice as a hockey player competing against boys.

"You've got your hockey skates for speed and maneuverability…your pads protecting your arms and legs and…finally your helmet. Hmmm…" Sonya pulls off her helmet as she finishes her last statement. Her ponytail falls down her back. "Here," she thrusts her helmet in my direction. I pinch the clip on the strap holding mine in place. The clasp pops apart. We trade helmets.

"That's much better. Thanks," I mutter grudgingly.

The helmet is still big, but not as big as Vinnie's had been. It is a definite improvement. Both of us look up as several Dragon players skate onto the ice from the other side of the arena. They all stand idly by, in the center of the ice, talking among themselves, as they wait for an informal team scrimmage to start. They are all watching

Sonya and I manage the helmet issue. Vinnie still stands along the boards watching from across the ice. I can only hear snippets of what they're saying in the huddle at center ice, but it's not hard imagining the rest.

"So, why is this new guy getting all her attention?" player #1 complains loud enough for Sonya and I to hear.

"That clown can't even skate," player #2 adds more quietly.

"Yah, let alone play hockey!" player #3 jokes.

"I haven't fallen down that many times in one day since I was five years old!" Player #4 demeans as they all look my way and laugh.

The players standing in the little gossip group shake their heads, then turn to rejoin their teammates in drills.

Sonya drops the puck on the ice in front of me, "Forget them, they're idiots sometimes. I want you to skate the puck past me," she challenges.

I take the puck awkwardly down the ice. I'm still steaming from the center ice team meeting, and not paying attention. Sonya suddenly comes up behind me, slamming me into the boards and stealing away the puck. In my surprise, I slip and go down again on the ice. "I'm sick of this!" I mutter angrily through clenched teeth. Sonya comes skating back in my direction executing a perfect hockey stop, wetting my face with ice shavings that spray off her blades.

"Is that the best you've got?!" she demands. I struggle to stand, leaning on my hockey stick for balance. "How does it feel to have someone take something from you?" comes her stiff and persistent question. I glare at her. She returns a withering look directly at me.

"You don't like me, do you?" I ask the obvious.

"I don't like thieves, especially one who steals from my uncle," Sonya answers with conviction. I struggle to regain my footing.

"Having problems?" she continues to ridicule.

"Look, I'm a street skater," I argue for some degree of credibility.

"Well then, maybe you belong back on the street," Sonya replies with disgust, as she tosses me the puck, "Catch!" I drop it, of course. "Nice hands. Maybe you should keep your eyes on the puck, and not on me," she complains.

"Who said I'm looking at you?" stings my icy comeback. We both stare each other down, displaying mutual dislike.

"Well, you were looking at me when you drew my picture making a goal. I found it on the floor near your hockey gear bag!" she argues.

I could feel my face burning from embarrassment that she had found my drawing of her. "How do you know it was you?" I volley back at her.

"Who else on this team has shoulder length black hair and wears a ponytail?" she smiles sarcastically.

If only I had thrown that stupid drawing away!

"Let's try a face-off," Sonya suggests.

"A what?" I have to ask. Sonya fakes a laugh born of disbelief.

"Gimme' a break. You don't even know what a face-off is?" she is relentless in her persecution.

"Sure, I just kind of… you know…get my sports mixed up. Basketball, football, hockey, soccer; just can't keep them all straight there are so many," I try to defend myself. Sonya rolls her eyes, not falling for my white lies.

"Put the puck on the ice," she orders. I do as she commands.

"Now you get on that side and I'll get on this side," comes her exasperated instructions.

I line up on my side of the puck. She lines up on her side of the puck.

"Ready? Now when I say, 'Go'… you try to get the puck back before I do," she blows out a breath and intentionally places her stick firmly in front of the puck with her hands gripping it tightly. "Okay?" she checks for my readiness. I eye the puck. Waiting for the word 'Go!' to scramble for control of it.

"No, better yet, you say, 'Go'," she waivers.

I utter an impatient sigh. Sonya places her stick just above and behind the puck. I mimic her every move.

"Okay… Say 'Go'," she reiterates.

"Go!" I shout.

Sonya reaches down and plucks the puck away even before I can move my stick. She is in control and skates away fast pushing the puck along with her stick toward the opposing net. In exasperation, I stand straight up and lean over my hockey stick looking directly over where Joe, Bernie, and Vinnie are looking on nervously.

"Well, so much for the championship!" Vinnie's remarks are loud enough for his voice to carry across the ice. I am ready to tear off my helmet and walk out! I see Joe and Bernie frown at Vinnie's words.

No Sir, he isn't getting the best of me…not yet! And neither is **she***!*

I ignore Vinnie's taunting, and skate awkwardly over to a defensive position in front of the goal. At that moment,

Sonya slaps at the puck. It's a hard Whack! The puck strikes me right between the legs. With a strangled yelp, my skates shoot out from under me. As I am going down, I hear a unified gasp from the other players on the team. I see Joe cringe as he starts toward the ice; Bernie and Vinnie are covering their faces. My head slams hard onto the ice. The stars dancing in my head disappear as the lights go out.

I'm not sure how long I've been out, but as I start to come to, it feels like I have been unconscious for hours. It's as though I have been in a long dark tunnel, struggling to get to the opening and daylight. My head hurts, and I feel throbbing pain in other, as yet undetermined, parts of my body. The images swimming behind my eyes are of my dad, as my mind fights to come back to the light. I hear his words plainly even though it is like he is floating in a cloud above my head, 'Work hard…Never quit… and…,' his face floats in and out as I struggle to keep him in one stationary place for focus, 'Always believe in yourself.' Slowly the ghostly image of my dad transforms into Joe Scagliotti leaning forward over my face, staring at me with worried concern.

"You okay, kid?" he asks anxiously.

"What happened?" I answer groggily, feeling the icy cold pack underneath my throbbing head.

"Your helmet slid off and your head hit the ice," Joe explains.

"Obviously you're not as hard headed as I thought," Bernie quips.

I am struggling to focus on the faces surrounding me as I lay flat on my back on the training table, still in full uniform, where someone had carried me after the lights went out. I slowly shift my gaze around the circle of faces peering out from behind hockey masks, my eyes settle on Sonya. She is standing at my feet, staring at the sizeable bump at my crotch; caused by an ice pack one of the trainers had shoved down the front of my hockey uniform pants, to keep down the swelling and numb the pain. I can now distinctly feel both between my legs. As I slowly realize what it is she continues staring at, I sit up in a flash!

I am cringing from the pain in my neck and the shot to my pride. I struggle off the training table and waddle out of the locker room as fast as I can go. My teammates, who had been surrounding the table only moments before, all erupt in laughter as I waddle out of the room. I am one sorry sight! The only face not laughing is Joe's. Inwardly, I appreciate the look of concern creasing his face as I brush by him out the door.

I hurry over to the bench behind the boards and yank the ice pack from the front of my hockey pants. I throw it on the bench. I sit down still feeling somewhat squeamish from the fall. Joe barks a command for certain players to take the ice. I stand to go, even though he has not called my name yet. "Anthony, you stay put. I don't think you are ready to scrimmage yet," Joe commands.

"I'm ready, Coach. I can do this. Put me in," I counter.

Joe walks over to me, lifts my chin to look into my eyes, and mutters, "Well, no dilation of the pupils, but if you start to feel woozy or sick, get off the ice immediately," he finishes with authority.

"Yes, Sir," my voice trails off as I step quickly out of the box and take the ice on shaky legs, with persistent throbbing throughout my body.

The scrimmage begins in earnest with three defenders to a side, and open goals. From the first drop of the puck it turns into one complete disaster. I can't stay on my feet. Balancing on my skates and controlling the puck at the same time proves too much for me in my condition. As I move down the ice on an open break, I discover the puck going in the opposite direction. I can't help but notice Joe and Bernie wiping their faces with their hands in frustration. At one point I hit the wall, and go down causing a collision and pile up. I look like one never ending blooper reel.

Joe shoves his hands in his pockets and heaves a sigh of frustration at the total ineptness he is witnessing on the ice when it comes to his team and their demonstrated hockey skills during this scrimmage. Bernie blows the whistle for me to come off the ice to the bench. My head is throbbing, I hurt all over, and my play time today is done.

"Take a break, Brooks. You're done for today," Joe orders. My mind runs through the days remaining before Joe has to have this team ready for the tournaments. Bernie and Joe look at each other reading what is in the other brother's heart and mind. It isn't hard to know what the two are thinking. *If the Ice Dragons are going to be contenders in this year's tournament, something is going to have to change…and fast!*

Joe remains genuinely worried over my fall on the ice. He keeps checking to see if my pupils are dilated. From my spot on the bench, through the remainder of the scrimmage I can tell that Joe does not like the way the other players are handling my discomfort. In their defense, they are reacting to the situation of one particular ice bag location rather than the fact that I am hurt, standoffish, and unfriendly. They don't care if I'm hurting, and I really don't care what they think, 'cuz I don't feel like talking. Only Joe and Bernie know the rest of the story when it comes to me and that's enough.

Afterward in the locker room Joe catches up with me,

"Hey kid, you hit your head hard and you can never be too careful when it comes to concussions from falls on the ice. Your mom needs to know about this and you need to see a doctor," Joe states authoritatively.

"Thanks, but I feel okay, and she has enough to worry about right now," I answer. "I was only out for a few minutes."

"Any amount of time a person is unconscious from a blow to the head is concerning. You were obviously struggling in that two play series after your fall. That's why I took you out. A day or two off to rest, after you see a doctor. No arguments," Joe finishes leaving no doubt about his intentions. I had to admit, the fall definitely had taken its toll on me.

Mom drives up to the back door of the ice arena. Joe follows me slowly over to the car. He had called Mom from his office to tell her about my fall on the ice and the head slam. She called the doctor right away, and was here to take me to see him and get my head checked out. Joe walks around the car to her open window and gives her the word on two days off if the doctor recommends it. Mom nods and before she drives off, thanks Joe for his concern about me, and the call home.

"Ma, what's the connection between Joe Scagliotti and my dad?" I ask with genuine curiosity and an edge to my voice, because I don't want to talk about my dad, but am curious about Joe. "I know there has to be more history there somewhere, besides that they went to school together. Joe sometimes acts like he knows things about Dad and us," I wait for her to explain.

"Well, I don't know everything. But this is some of what I do know from things your Nana and dad have told me. Joe and Dad knew each other as boys in high school. Joe is a couple years older than your dad. Joe's notoriety for playing hockey made him lots of friends. Living in the same neighborhood for most of their lives, Joe and your dad were bumping into each other on a regular basis. They were not just casual friends," she continues explaining. "There were family connections, too. Joe's dad and Gramps had worked together at the Ford Plant before Antonio, the elder Mr. Scagliotti, retired to run the pizzeria," Mom slows as she shares her observation, "Gramps and Antonio were good friends."

"Does Joe have a family? He never mentions anyone but his brother Bernie, and his niece and nephew, Sonya and Vinnie," I persist in asking.

"Not sure, but I don't think so. Nana mentioned what a shame it is him not having children of his own, 'cuz he would make a great father," Mom says with conviction as we pull into the doctor's office parking lot.

"Well, you just never know about people, do ya'?" I quietly conclude.

"No, you really don't, not until you take the time to look inside," then Mom turns off the car, looking at me with sad, pleading eyes.

CHAPTER FOURTEEN

I arrive at work right on time. I have been bussing tables for the last half hour without a let up. My head is still aching some from my fall on the ice during the scrimmage. I've been off of practice since then, but both Mom and Joe insisted on it. Didn't figure I'd win with both of them on the same side, opposite me.

"Anthony!" Joe calls from behind the counter, standing near the cash register, waving me over. "Come here!"

"Be right there," I answer, collecting the dirty plates from off the last table in this section, and dropping them into the bus cart with a clatter. I push the cart over to the opposite wall out of the way, and roll over to Joe still standing at the register.

"I want to show you how to work the cash register," Joe explains.

I shrug my shoulders in wonderment, "Why?" I ask.

"It's like the slap shot. You never know when you'll have to use it," he smiles showing his silver tooth.

Joe begins showing me the key features on the cash register. I feign listening carefully to his instruction, but I'm thinking, *Just why is he trusting me? Especially after what I did to earn this sentence of slavery. He does seem to enjoy watching my courtroom consequence carried out in his service.*

We both turn to the opening of the door and the sound of the cowbell clanging loudly, announcing an incoming customer.

T.J. and his pals approach Joe and me, still standing behind the counter.

"What can I get you fellas?" Joe asks cordially.

T.J. and I give each other ominous looks. T.J. shifts his attention to Sonya in the kitchen.

"I'd like something hot, spicy, and extra saucy," T.J. speaks loudly enough, so Sonya could not help but hear his order. All his guys laugh and jab each other in the ribs ogling Sonya who stays in the kitchen and refuses to look their way. I press my lips together, mustering every ounce of self-control I have, staring at T.J. with a scorching glare.

"That would be our Red-Line Power Play," Joe informs T.J.

"Whatever you say, old man," T.J. returns, as Joe scribbles the order on the ticket slip, clipping it to the line above the kitchen window, ignoring T.J.'s disrespectful address. Sonya grabs it off the clip with a snap.

Joe informs T.J., "That'll be…," as his eyes drop to the bottom of the duplicate order slip, "Twelve ninety-five," he finishes without his usual smile.

T.J. pulls out a wad of cash from his pocket. Joe eyes the bills. T.J. peels bills off and drops them on the counter. As he does so, Joe proceeds to show me how the cash register works, with no particular concern over making T.J. wait for his change.

"First, you enter the amount of the order on the keys," Joe explains.

I look hesitantly at T.J. wishing that Joe would stop

teaching me how to use the cash register at this particular moment in time. I want him to give T.J. his change, and finish the tutorial on the cash register after these neighborhood pirates depart for other waters. But no luck, so I follow Joe's instructions.

"Then push the Enter button," he continues.

I press the key. Click! The drawer opens with the cash. Joe proceeds, showing me how to make change as I see T.J., out of the corner of my eye, checking out what's in the cash drawer. I hand the correct change to T.J., who happens to be staring at me with a cold calculating grin on his face.

Sonya calls out, "Anthony!" and hands the hot and ready Red-Line Power Play Pizza to me through the serving window, keeping her eyes glued to mine. I hand the boxed pizza to T.J.

"Yah, guess we'll be seeing ya' around, Shorty," T.J. quips with specific emphasis on his pet name for me. "We'll be back again for that hot, spicy, extra saucy dish," he finishes by clicking his tongue at the corner of his mouth for emphasis, and winking his eye toward the direction of the kitchen.

T.J. offers a sneering laugh. Sonya gives T.J. a return withering glare that is unmistakable in its meaning and intention to deliver a stabbing rebuke.

"Good riddance to that riff-raff!" Joe muttered angrily as the bell jingled with the slamming of the door.

Finally, after a few days off, my no practice sentence is up. It is the third day after hitting my head on the ice, and I am on my way to practice. I have promised myself that today will be better. I still am feeling the effects of the bump on my head. I still have a swollen bump, and the head slam, according to the doctor, had caused a minor concussion. The doc had ordered two days off the ice with lots of rest, and limited activity. The bad part had been the nagging headache, but now even that seemed to be disappearing. At this moment, my biggest concern is not making a fool of myself again.

The players, fully suited up, are on the ice by the time I dash from Mom's car and hurry into the ice arena, slightly late. The other players on my team are skating around idly, some stretching, some standing and chatting waiting for the practice to begin. I race out to Joe, Bernie, and Sonya standing center ice.

"You're late!" Joe accuses.

"I know. Sorry Coach," I apologize.

"No excuses," Joe persists.

"I say we start with laps, a lot of them," Bernie suggests loudly.

"Forget laps," Joe snaps as he blows the whistle and calls the team over, acting miffed about something.

"In fact, forget practice!" comes Joe's taut reply, as his players skate over to him, mystified about what has him so worked up.

"Go back to the locker room and get dressed," Joe looks around the circle of perplexed faces belonging to his players. "The Red Wings are in town. I got us tickets in the second row behind the players' bench!"

The Detroit Dragons break out in cheers and high-fives. No complaints whatsoever about the return to the locker room and stashing the gear back in the bags. I lag behind trailing Joe off the ice.

"Real hockey? The NHL?" I ask in disbelief at our good fortune.

"Sometimes you learn by doing and sometimes you learn best by watching," Joe finishes as Sonya stands counting all the players at practice that day. You could see her logical mind adding up the cost of Joe's generous gesture. Everyone knows that NHL tickets aren't cheap!

"But, counting Anthony, there are nine of us," Sonya argues defensively.

Joe takes out a wad of tickets from his pocket and begins to fan them out for all of his players to see. He then glances over to me and winks.

"Don't worry, kid. I got this covered," he flashes his smile at Sonya.

"Joe is driving and so am I, so decide who you are riding with," Bernie announces excitedly. "This 'bus' is leavin' for the Joe Louis Arena!"

I had never been to a real live NHL Hockey game before. The arena is packed as Joe leads us down the aisle to seats in front. All of my teammates seem to know exactly what to do. I can't stop watching everything going on around me. I don't want to miss a thing!

Joe leans over the barrier rail and shouts down the length of the players' bench, "Hey, Guys!" All the Red Wing players turn and look in his direction with smiles, waves, and nods acknowledging Joe's presence.

We all stare, speechless, at Henrik Zetterberg, chosen as The Most Valuable Player of the 2008 Stanley Cup Playoffs. He actually smiles and inquires in a most friendly way, "What's happening, Joe?"

I watch with amazement as Joe Scagliotti, personally interacts with Hank Zetterberg on the Red Wings' bench.

"I brought my Dragons, Hank. Show them how the pros play the game," Joe teases.

"You got it, Joe!" Zetterberg assures with a thumbs up.

Incredible that I got to witness, with my own eyes, Joe Scagliotti interacting with the Red Wings and their star player, Hank Zetterberg. Yes, I remember hearing the sports' headlines and some of the names at the breakfast table when the Wings were in town, or winning the Stanley Cup. Wow! Joe knows all the Red Wings? They sure act like they know him. Sonya, sitting beside me, follows my stare down the players' bench to where my eyes remain glued to Hank Zetterberg.

"Well, where do you think all these tickets came from?" she snorts with her usual measure of contempt. "They sure don't grow on trees!"

Both Sonya and I redirect our attention to center ice, as the game gets underway. The puck drops and the game is on! I am totally into the action and cheering for the Red Wings. The excitement is pumping me up and I feel a real part of the team we came to watch! As Joe, Bernie, Sonya and Vinnie sit around me, explaining some of the finer points of the game, I am beginning to feel part of this team, too. We are the Dragon's. Our hockey season will be made or broken together.

"Watch how Zetterberg handles the stick. He always keeps his head up," Joe pointed out. I nod.

"You got to be aware of what's happening around you on the ice, without looking at the puck," Sonya offers. I nod, again.

"She's right. If you stare at the puck while skating, someone's gonna' nail you," Vinnie warns.

I turn to Vinnie and smile, "Thanks. And thanks for letting me use your equipment and skates."

Vinnie doesn't let down his guard, but continues to stare out onto the ice. "You just make sure you get us to the championship," he warns without looking at me. *So much for my momentary break through with Vinnie!* I turn my attention back to the play and the action on the ice.

Within minutes, an opposing player checks one of the Red Wings' players. He slams into the wall right in front of where our team is sitting. The Red Wings' player goes down, gets back on his feet, tears off his gloves and his helmet, and punches the other player.

Joe smiles at me showing off his silver-capped tooth, "It's 'Captain Crunch' time!"

No sooner did Joe utter those words, than the ensuing fist fight turns into an all-out brawl. Other players skate over and join the melee. I watch, with shock, but the thrill of the game has me in its grip. There sure is something about this sport!

All the way home Sonya, Vinnie, Joe and I talk non-stop about the Red Wings' game we had just witnessed. We all agree that in order for the Dragons to make the championship game, we all will have to work extra hard helping each other. Sonya and Vinnie are certain that with some extra coaching and more practice, I should be able to pick up the skating skills and hockey moves needed to help take us into the tournaments. With Joe's prompting, we all rededicate ourselves to seeing this through and earning a chance for the Detroit Ice Dragons to play in the championship game. I am more determined than ever to get my team to that spot.

I charge into my house following the Wings' game. Joe drops me off last. I toss my jacket on the hook in the hall. As I come into the living room, Mom is watching the 11:00 news and Nana is knitting in her chair.

"Where you been, young man? You got any idea how late it be?" Nana quizzes.

"Been to a riot!" I respond with excitement, and a smile. Nana drops her knitting, "In the streets?!" she exclaims.

Mom, who suddenly perks up, looks at her mother with disbelief.

"No, at Joe Louis Arena!" I counter, thinking I'll head for my bedroom downstairs. "It was awesome!" I call over my shoulder. "Joe said it was 'Captain Crunch Time'!"

It isn't hard to tell that Mom and Nana are excited to see me cranked up about something. It has been awhile since I've cared enough to talk about much of anything that took more than two words. Their attention is now completely on me.

"Now why would anyone want to go into a hockey rink to riot?" Nana shrugs her shoulders and resumes knitting. "Hmmm… just can't figure what gets into these young kids today," she continues puzzling the whole idea.

Mom is chuckling to herself at Nana's somewhat skewed observation about modern day young people.

"Ma, you are something else," she teases. "Glad you had a good time, Anthony. It is nice to see you smile again," Mom calls out after me.

I let it go. I don't feel like arguing the point tonight. I did have a good time. It had been a great game. I was really into watching the action on the ice. It was stuff made of dreams and wishes. Hockey was becoming a game that I knew I could be good at with more practice. I just knew it!

Later in the week, I ask Mom to drop me off at the ice arena so that I can practice during free skate time. She has some errands to run on this side of town, so it works out well for me and her. I didn't say anything to anyone else about the extra practice, because I really didn't want many people around. Maybe I can practice my basic skating skills without looking like an idiot. I lace up my skates tight, and hit the ice. I am beginning to enjoy the quiet time on the ice. It is fairly quiet with not many people around. I am so intent on my practice, that I don't see Joe and Sonya enter the ice arena. I am too busy working on my game.

I have been taking shots from various distances and angles, for almost half an hour. I am missing many shots. Some are deflecting off the plastic safety barrier just a few feet away, and some are flying into the stands. I am feeling discouraged about how inconsistent my shots seem to be.

I hear a voice call out loudly, "Doesn't this embarrass you?" I turn to face the all too familiar voice, consistently testy since the robbery. I look in the direction of the sound, not surprised to find Sonya leaning out over the barrier in front of the players' bench.

"What?" I snap back, skating to a stop fifteen feet from her.

"This!" Sonya states spreading her arms out to encompass the ice and me on it. I turn my back on her biting remarks, position myself in front of the net, and swing my stick, with even greater determination.

CHAPTER FIFTEEN

he tiny black puck flies into the net! "Score!" I shout with glee. James is standing on the other side of the hockey game table, no smile to be seen. "That's whack!" James pouts as I lick the tip of my index finger and make an imaginary slash in the air.

"No, that's a slap shot!" I brag, retrieving the tiny puck from the back of James' goalie net. "You think that's good, wait 'til you see me play **real** hockey!" I finish with a triumphant fist pump.

James stands fixed to his spot, with a completely stunned expression on his face. "You play hockey?" he asks in disbelief. I nod with satisfaction.

"Street hockey?" James continues trying to make sense of what I had just revealed to him.

"Ice hockey," I answer.

James shakes his head questioningly. Still dumbfounded by what I had just told him. "I think I will stick to basketball," James mumbles.

"Well at least with hockey, I'll get a chance to play," I explain. "I'm not tall like you. I will always be outgunned on the basketball court. With hockey, I feel like I have a chance to contribute more to my team and the game," I finish putting words to my feelings.

"Man, Bro…I had no idea you were playing real ice

hockey. No wonder you are never at home when I come by. How long's this been goin' on? Your Ma never said a word 'bout you puttin' on the blades. All the while I was thinkin' you was still hurtin' bad over your dad, or busy workin' off your court debt."

"Didn't really want anyone else to know. Besides, I have been workin' off my debt, this is all part of it. I wanted to be sure I could play the game, before I told you that I was on the team. This ice hockey is a whole new game!" It felt good finally sharing this with James. I had needed to be in control of something, since nothing else in my life seemed that way.

James is still recovering from his shock that I would play ice hockey rather than basketball. My 'Mister Big Shot' days have been my passion and obsession. No one knows that better than James. I have worked hard over the last several weeks of practice, and I am finally feeling like I am getting to the point where I could start to make a difference for my team. I am more confident that I will not embarrass myself in front of my friends and teammates with my skill level of play.

"So, James want to come with me and watch the team scrimmage tomorrow after school?" I ask with enthusiasm. "I'm sure Coach won't mind if you come along. We'll skate over to the pizzeria after school and hitch a ride to the ice arena with Joe," I suggest with optimism.

"Sure, I would like that. Watching you play ice hockey, that is," James finishes quietly. "I just wish you trusted me enough to tell me."

I could never explain to James what I have been through and am still dealing with every hour of every day.

144

He can't fully understand, because he has never had to endure something like losing his dad. Knowing that one of the people you love and trust more than anyone else in the world, died committing a criminal act, is devastating. I hope he never has to know that kind of pain.

"Great! Tomorrow then! Meet me after the last bell by the stoop at the front entrance. We will skate over together. And thanks, James," I finish with a pat on his back. "You're the best!"

First Team Scrimmage

Joe, Vinnie, Sonya, and the rest of the team are all seated on the Dragon's team bench. James sits in the bleachers with the other spectators, three rows above the bench well behind the nets and glass. I look up to see his thumbs up signal as I warm up skating the length of the ice board on our side of the arena. I raise my hockey stick to signal I have seen him. We both smile at each other. I am hoping to have the best game of my short career on the ice. Bernie, with whistle in mouth, is on the ice directing and refereeing the team scrimmage.

The Detroit Ice Dragons are divided into two teams for the scrimmage. The White Dragons, my team for the scrimmage, wear white jerseys. The Black Dragons, my opponents for the scrimmage, wear black jerseys. Both teams are wearing the same Ice Dragon hockey pants.

Bernie calls the teams to center ice for the drop. Both teams position themselves to gain the advantage. Sticks in place, gear snapped and zipped, with skates laced and at the ready. Bernie blows the whistle, drops the puck in the middle of the center circle, and the game is on!

I fight for the puck, along with my team. Yes, we get possession! The White Dragons have the puck and are quickly skating into the Black Dragons' zone. A White Dragon player passes the puck to me in the center. I blast a tremendous slap shot. The puck zips across the ice toward the goal. The opposing Black Dragon goalie makes a terrific stop in the butterfly stance. Bernie blows the whistle. No luck! No score!

"Great Shot, Anthony!" Bernie yells, after dropping the whistle from his mouth. Joe begins motioning me over to the bench with wild arm waves. I skate over, out of breath.

"Yah, Coach?" I pant gasping for air. Joe throws his arm over my shoulder.

"Listen son, you're making great progress out there!" Joe leans in closer. "But if you want to get even more power on your shots, you've got to follow through completely. Okay?"

"Okay, you got it, Coach," I reply still breathing hard, as I lean over to rest my hands on my knees. I can't help but see Joe turn to Sonya and smile.

I turn and skate quickly back out onto the ice, rejoining my teammates, feeling like I have just opened a present.

The scrimmage continues for more than an hour. Everyone is tired when it ends, but Joe and Bernie seem happier than they have been since the season's start. Even Sonya is being nicer than usual, smiling and talking more than I'm used to seeing. Vinnie still seems out of sorts, but I know it is probably killing him to be unable to help out his team and take the ice as he is used to doing.

James hurries down from his perch in the bleachers as soon as the last whistle blows, and the players exit the ice.

"Awesome, Dude!" James spills out his words and can't stop talking. This was his first hockey game in person, and he was as excited as I had been the first time I sat through a live hockey game.

"I can't believe how fast you move, and how hard you slap the puck with your stick! Man, where did you learn those moves...dodging in and out between players? That high sticking stuff is rough!! No wonder they fight all the time during NHL games on T.V.! A guy could get killed out there!! Really, Shooter you are great on the ice!!" James finishes out of breath from talking so fast.

"Thanks, James but I still have a lot to learn. I'm lucky to have such good coaches," I smile as I point my stick at Vinnie and Sonya, standing nearby. They both smile back. Now that was a change for the better!

"Hey James, maybe you want to take up the sport?" Sonya teases.

"Thanks, but no. I'm sticking to basketball. Much safer!" James admits and everyone laughs.

With my athletic gear bag in one hand, hockey stick in the other, and James walking beside me, we stroll out of the arena. The two of us stand by the back exit wall, waiting for Mom to pick us up.

"You're really good at this game, Shooter!" James praises.

"Well, I have improved quite a bit with all the practicing I've been doing, but I need to be on my best game by the playoffs. I'm hoping if you come to watch me play, you will really see something great!" I state with as much confidence as I can manage. "I hope to be kickin' some serious booty, in this sport!" I beam proudly.

"Well, just like in basketball there's a big difference between practices and games," James reasons logically.

Suddenly, a long black car, older model Buick, pulls up in front of the back entrance to the ice arena. It sure isn't my mother. All the car doors open and about five guys pile out.

"Hey Shorty!" comes the familiar, chilling greeting. James and I watch as T.J. and his thugs gather around the two of us in a semi-circle. T.J. shoves me hard against the wall of the building.

"Hey!" I protest loudly, dropping my bag of gear.

"We don't want any trouble," James states with a steady voice. T.J.'s gorillas grab James by his shirt, restraining him.

"Then shut up!" T.J. warns grabbing me by the throat and not letting go. "Dude!" T.J. grins mischievously.

I feel like I am choking. I can't breathe!

"What are you doing switching teams on me?" T.J. turns to his buddies and lets out a fake laugh. "You can't just dip off my team!" T.J. squeezes my throat tighter. I begin to cough and choke. "Not without paying!" T.J. snarls.

I continue coughing, as James begins struggling against his captors and takes a stiff slug to the gut by one of the smaller guys restraining him. James buckles to his knees. T.J. releases his hold on my neck. I begin to breathe again. I can feel the heat in my face and the pounding of my heart.

"I, uh...already paid," I croak.

"I believe Shorty here thinks he's bigger than he really is!" T.J. challenges as he slugs me in the mid-section. My gut takes the blow and I fall to my knees, rolling over onto my side with my knees drawn up.

"Ouuu…wahhh!" sounds of pain gush from my mouth.

"Now listen up, lil' man. Tomorrow, you're going to clean out the pizza man's cash register," T.J. snarls with authority.

"I won't do it!" I vow through clenched teeth.

T.J. grabbed my hockey stick from atop my gear bag, "What did you say?" He jammed the blade of the stick up against my throat. I hear James starting to struggle again against T.J.'s thugs. I hear a kick and James cries out.

"You'll do it, or you'll end up like your old man!" T.J. spews out his venomous warning, as he throws my hockey stick to the ground and turns to leave with his buddies. They all pile back into the black car and speed off. I stagger to my feet and struggle over to where James is still lying on the ground moaning.

"James, James you okay?" I ask anxiously, still feeling the ache of the punch in my gut. At the moment, I'm not much help. We both are slow to recover from the vicious ambush.

"Yah, I think I'm still alive," comes James' angry reply. "What makes those creeps think they can rule the world?!" James demands as he continues to keep his spot on the ground. He stretches out his legs and complains loudly. "Those goons are goin' to get theirs and you can take that to the bank! That shrimp who kicked me is never going to be taller than I am! Just wait and see, the day is coming when I'll kick his sorry hide clear downtown! He'll be gettin' his!"

Thankfully by the time Mom pulls up in the car for the ride home, we are both on our feet, brushed off, and looking none the worse for wear. As I load my gear into the trunk of the car, I turn to check out footsteps I hear. I see Joe walking back inside the rear door to the ice arena. I never saw or heard him come out earlier. It sent a strange sensation up my spine. *Had Joe seen any of what had gone down between me, James and T.J.'s hoodlums? What had he heard? It didn't matter. There was no way I would ever be taking a penny from Joe Scagliotti again.*

Our talk, all the way home in the car, is only about the team scrimmage. James and I never mention one word to my mother about the scrimmage that had taken place outside the ice arena. We talk only of the scrimmage held inside the Scagliotti Ice Arena, and how it had all turned out.

CHAPTER SIXTEEN

*I*t is quiet in the basement. I am concentrating hard on the plays I'm executing on my hockey table. I am tired from the long day at school, the two hours at the pizzeria, and practice with Sonya and Vinnie. Joe drove us all home around 7:00. Maybe it is the spinning and sliding of the cut-out hockey players I have been maneuvering up and down the table, hitting the tiny puck for scores that keep the game going on and on. Whatever the reason, I am feeling drowsy and hearing a repeated echo inside my head. The voice of my father, "Work hard…never quit…and always believe in yourself." In defiance of the same message and trying hard to wipe it from my mind, I rotate the player controlling the puck, shoot the puck to center ice, and manage to pull out the stops and slap shot the puck into the goalie net. Score! *How's that for wiping out the voices?!*

Suddenly I hear Nana yelling from upstairs, "Anthony, dinner's ready. Wash up and get to the table," I look up, no ghostly image, no voices inside my head. I took the stairs two at a time and arrived at the table shortly after washing my hands at the kitchen sink. Nana and Mom were both waiting patiently for me to be seated.

"What were ya' doin' down there?" Nana asks with interest.

I take a bite of corn before answering. "Playing table hockey, but I also play on a team," I inform, looking at Nana.

She raises her brow and asks, "A hockey team. You mean on ice?" I nod. Not speaking while I chew my barbecued ribs.

"Why the sudden interest in hockey?" I shrug at her question.

"I don't know," I say wiping the sweet sauce from my mouth.

"Then why? Why are you playing hockey of all things?"

"Because I'm too short to play basketball."

"I'm all for it!" Mom replies looking encouragingly at me.

"You're all for it until he takes a puck in the chops! I've seen those hockey players," Nana snaps back. "Honest to goodness, I have more teeth than they do."

"Ma, they have mouth pieces," Mom argues.

"So do I!" Nana announces popping out her dentures.

"Gross!" I moan.

"Mother! We're eating!" Mom protests.

Nana shoves her false teeth back into her mouth. She stands up abruptly from the table and starts clearing the dishes.

"After dinner your mom and I are going to visit your uncle," Nana stops and looks directly at me. "Would you like to come along, Anthony?"

I start to open my mouth to protest but am stopped by Mom's interruption, "He wants to see you."

"Well, I don't want to see him, ever!" I shout

emphatically, jumping up from my chair and leaving the kitchen without a backward glance, because that's how mad I am at the very suggestion.

Later in the Week

It is Thursday. One more day until the weekend, and one last swipe of the inside of Joe's Pizzeria's front window with the cleaning rag and window spray. I look out and see T.J. and his crew drive by slowly. T.J. and I lock eyes, followed by a mean sneer from T.J. as the guys in the backseat hang out the windows trash talking. I quickly finish the last corner, gather my window washing tools and head for the back room. I'm relieved to have a door with a bell between me and the street. The edgy feeling I always experience whenever T.J. makes an appearance dogs me the rest of the afternoon.

About an hour later, while I wipe the tables in the front dining room, Joe limps past me with a pizza box, heading for the front door.

"Anthony, I've got to deliver this pizza. Can you watch the store for a minute?" Joe half asks, half commands as he glances over his shoulder.

"I...I...," comes my uncertain stammering.

"I'm only dropping it off next door," Joe turns halfway out the door,

"I will be right back," his voice trails off as the door closes behind him.

I walk to the window to look out and see if the "Trouble" is still around. The image of T.J. and his pirates keeps running over and over in my head, like a movie that never ends: Riding around in that big black car, hanging

153

out the windows, yelling and laughing at people on the street as they roll by, spreading their own version of terror around 'the hood'.

I look over at the few customers scattered about the restaurant. Everyone is otherwise occupied. No one is watching or anywhere near the front checkout counter. Without another thought I walk over behind the front counter and pop open the cash register drawer. I start to reach into the drawer to pull out the cash and notice my Ice Dragon sketch. Joe has it displayed on the wall alongside other famous National Hockey League jerseys. I pull my hand out of the cash drawer, close the cash register with a quiet click, and walk to the kitchen to get the broom. The floors would need a good sweep before closing time.

I walk in the door of the pizzeria at 10:00 A.M. on Saturday, as Joe had requested on the phone last night. It is one of the earliest shifts Joe has asked me to fill in at least a month.

"'The early bird gets the worm'" as they say, Joe quips with a big smile that shows his silver tooth. "You're ridin' with me, so let's get in the truck," Joe announces heading for the back door of the shop.

"What is goin' on? I thought I was workin' the early shift today," I question with a slight annoyance in my voice.

"You are workin', just not at the store," Joe smiles as he tosses me the gear bag he has stashed in the backroom. I caught it in mid-air. "We got a big tournament coming up, a little work on the ice will do you good...do us all

154

good," Joe finished as I followed him out the rear door to the truck.

"Well, you better be counting this as some of the money I still owe you, so as I can get this debt paid off and not have to sling pizza anymore," I object.

"You got it kid!" Joe chimes as he starts the truck and I jump in beside him. "Hey, want an ice cream on the way?" he counters trying to improve my mood.

"At 10:00 in the morning? I don't think so, but maybe later." We drove the rest of the way to the ice arena making small talk. Mostly, Joe making small talk and me listening. Things are definitely changing between us, and for the better. Joe tells me about some of his days playing hockey for the Wings. He doesn't usually talk about it much, but he was today.

"Yes Sir, your teammates are your strength. You count on them when there is no one else to lean on. Most are great, like brothers. Those were the days, when you knew who had your back, no matter what!" Joe lectured as he parked the truck in the usual place, near the rear door facing out, so he didn't have to back up. No other cars are parked in the lot, so we have the rink to ourselves. I grab the gear bag from the floor of the truck and we walk to the back door together. It was looking as though it would be some one-on-one ice time with just Joe and me. Joe doesn't bother to stop and unlock the back door as he usually does. We just walk inside. This is weird!

As usual, it took a minute for my eyes to adjust to the dark interior of the building. The lights were already on over the rink when we step into the hall. We walk in silence to the boards in front of the home bench. I throw down the gear bag, starting to suit up. It is quiet on this side of the arena, but I can hear someone skating on the other side. No voices, weird again!

I sail out into the middle of the ice holding my stick in front of me. I throw down the puck, turning in circles, working my stick back and forth guiding the puck as I go. I start pushing the puck with speed and control, skating to the opposite end of the rink. I repeat this practice warm-up…up and down, and back again, four times trying to increase my speed and still control the puck as I fly around the sides and across the middle of the ice. I'm skating idly now to catch my breath, my back to the bench, where I know Joe is watching every move of my warm-up drills. I am using my stick to knock the frozen crystals off from my skates. It is the build-up that always comes with flashing the edges, cutting the ice with your blades and making the ice crystals fly, so they stick to every part of your skate.

"Gimme' the stick!" I jump at the sound of Sonya's voice. "Wow, jumpy aren't we?" she teases as she grabs the hockey stick from my gloved hand.

"What are **you** doin' here? Where did **you** come from?" my still surprised questions roll out with more disdain than I intend.

"Workin', just like you! Or so Uncle Joe says! Well, this is work all right!" she continues complaining. "I'm about to show you the correct way to do a slap shot, Mister!" With that, Sonya starts grabbing my hands and placing them on the stick to show a proper hold. "Hold your hands like this and stay even with the puck!" She places her hands over mine pressing down hard on the hockey stick. She begins pushing my shoulders down toward the ice shamelessly, like I'm some little kid. I was steaming mad! I grit my teeth, keeping my cool. I am not showing her that it bothers me one little bit!

"Stay low. Bend at the waist. Let your shoulders create a line toward the goal," she demonstrates for my benefit. "Right elbow up," she continues modeling as she lines up the puck. "Follow through, but with your shoulders," Sonya takes the stick along with me, her hands over mine, standing cheek-to-cheek, side by side, and swings the hockey stick to make contact with the puck through the practice shot.

"How's that feel?" Sonya asks with her face against mine.

"Great! Um…Good," I stammer embarrassed by the effect she was having on me.

Sonya immediately steps back with a disgusted look on her face, picking up on my meaning.

"Now, you try it. Remember to keep your head down, your shoulders low and square, and follow through," she commands.

I line up the puck on the ice.

"A little more to the left," Sonya continues to dictate.

I adjust the stick a little to the left.

"A little to the right now," another adjustment at her command.

More out of anger than skill, I slap a smooth hard stroke directly at the puck and to my surprise it is a beauty: A hard, line drive into the net; strong, straight, and sure.

"Perfect," and for the first time Sonya smiles approvingly right at me.

For another hour I keep practicing the routine. *How could such small things like 'stay low, right elbow up, keep your shoulders square, and follow through in the set-up,' make such a big difference?*

I keep repeating her words over and over inside my head. Most of the shots go in, only a few deflect off the frame of the goal. Suddenly, even the misses are in the direct vicinity of the intended target. Progress to say the least!

Sonya and Joe are standing over by the sideboard talking to each other. Joe has not stopped smiling for the last half hour. I am still mad, but how can I argue with the outcome? It is definitely working.

Sonya comes skating over after a few more of my practice shots to the net. "Yah, well don't go getting a big head either! Doing it here with no pressure is not the same as in a game when defenders are all over you. You have to concentrate and keep your head in the game. Be aware of who and what is going on around you, but don't let it shut you down. Do what you know works, like what I have shown you," she finishes with superiority.

"Yah, well what makes you such an expert on the slap shot?" I challenge, letting my anger take its course.

"Check the stats from last year, Rookie!" she fumes as she skates off the ice.

On the ride back to the pizzeria it was just Joe and me in the truck. I ask Joe about the stats from last season's Detroit Area Junior Girls' Hockey League and the record number of successful slap shots made. It isn't what I want to hear. Sonya finished second in the girls' league with sixteen, just behind Vinnie's stats for slap shots in the Junior Boys' League with 18. Ouch!

Practice Continues

Mom drops me off at the ice arena, while she goes to visit a sick friend at Mercy Hospital. She says I will have a couple of hours to practice and then she will wait outside for however long it takes for me to finish. She brought a book to read and won't mind the wait. Mom is always so great about waiting for me to practice and work on my game.

I am lugging my hockey stick and equipment bag out of the locker room and into the arena. Our impromptu practice is over, but some of the guys are still hanging around for some additional time on the ice. The arena is practically empty, except for our Ice Dragon players. A number of the guys on our team have met for more than an hour and we have just finished up this extra, unscheduled practice. We like playing pickup games with two sides: Supplying pressure for shots and defense really steps up everyone's game. Tonight, Joe did some one-on-one coaching with some of the guys. They are still going at it out on the ice. Joe just never seems to tire of hockey.

I'm walking aimlessly toward the hall that leads to the outside door, and thinking that I will be waiting awhile for mom to arrive. I am approaching the massive double doors leading to the figure skating arena across from the hockey rink. I decide to check out the source of sound that reveals someone is skating there. The bright lights beam down directly onto the ice, and there is no mistaking the skater. *What in the world is Sonya doing figure skating? She hadn't been at the team practice that just ended. Had she been here all this time?* I watch from a distance, without her knowing I'm there. She has on a skirted, pink, lace figure skating outfit instead of the raggedy hockey uniform, I usually see her in. Sonya is in the middle of a spin, head back, with her dark hair streaming behind her and one arm reaching toward the ceiling, a definition of gracefulness.

I quickly pull the sketchpad out of the outside pocket on my hockey bag. I grab the pencil out of my pocket and start drawing immediately the vision before me. I have never really sketched anyone skating before. Trying to capture, in a drawing, such graceful movement in only a moment is a challenge. Sonya is as perfect in her execution of the spin as Sarah Hughes in the Winter Olympics. When Sonya comes out of her spin, she drifts backwards effortlessly, fist pumping and squealing in triumph. She appears lost in her own world, sailing around the ice like a floating balloon on a soft summer breeze. She starts skating straight ahead with speed and explodes into a double axel jump without a hitch. She lands perfectly and in total control. Her squeal of accomplishment is drowned out by my loud and deafening crack of applause, as I walk into view. I shove my detailed drawing into the outside pocket of my bag, and stash the sketchpad and pencil into the open flat flap on the bag. I shut it with a quick zip.

Sonya skates over to me, now standing behind the board on the sidelines.

"You're really good!" I say honestly and with earnest.

Sonya grabs the towel draped over the rink boards. She towels herself off as if this were an everyday occasion.

"You think I'm good, you should have seen my mother

160

skate," she proclaims with pride, trying to catch her breath. "She was a world-class skater," she adds tossing the towel back over the boarded wall.

"Can I ask you a question?" I proceed with caution.

"Sure. What is it?" Sonya complies.

"What happened to her? How did she die?" I boldly ask wanting to know something more about this girl and her story.

"She was doing a triple axel and had an aneurism," Sonya responds quietly blowing out an emotional breath. "She died on the ice."

"At least she died doing what she loved," I offer with sympathy.

"Want to see a picture of her? I always carry it with me for inspiration," Sonya reaches up and snaps open the heart-shaped gold and red-stoned locket around her neck, not really waiting for me to respond. She holds it up for me to see. "I skate for her, and for me. Dad gave me her necklace to wear when I turned seven and started skating. I've worn it ever since," Sonya concludes with a sigh.

Looking back at me from the tiny photograph is a beautiful young woman with long dark hair and dark eyes, who bears an uncanny resemblance to Sonya. The young woman in the photo has on a bright yellow and red-skirted costume that fits her perfectly and shows off a tiny waist and long slender legs. Around her neck hangs a shiny silver medal on a red, white, and blue ribbon. Hanging just inside the ribbon and dangling down above the award is the very same heart-shaped necklace with the red stones, that Sonya is now showing to me."

"Wow! She must have been good! What did she do to win the medal?" I ask curiously.

"Mom was a U.S.A. National's Finalist: Runner-Up that year."

"Only the best skaters make it to those competitions!" I praise with a new found appreciation for just how hard it is to compete at those levels and win.

"This picture was taken two years before she died. I was five, Vinnie was eight. I miss having a mother, especially one as beautiful as mine," tears glisten at the corner of Sonya's eyes.

We both stand silently staring down at the picture of Sonya's and Vinnie's mother. She really was beautiful. No wonder her children were skaters, obviously they had a natural ability for it.

"How did practice go tonight?" Sonya asks wanting to change the subject.

"It was good. We seem to be skating more as a team and anticipating what other Dragon players are thinking. That has to help," I add trying to keep away from the talk of her mother.

"Wait up? It will only take me a few minutes to change. We can walk out together." Then Sonya finishes with another question, "You got that slap shot perfected yet?" she is skimming over the fact that she had just asked me to wait for her.

"Getting close," I answer. We both smile at each other. She turns, and walks into the locker room with her bag.

I pull out my small sketch pad and pencil again. I continue sketching my idea of what Sonya had looked like skating so gracefully only moments before. I outline her doing her triple spin. It looks good for a five minute sketch. I'd finish later.

Sonya is true to her word, and in only a few minutes, we were walking toward the back door, which leads out of the arena.

"Someone picking you up?" Sonya asks.

I hate saying so, but, "Yah, my mom is coming by in a while to give me a lift home. You hungry?" *Why I am asking her that, I have no idea!*

"Uh…sure. I'm always starving after practice," she sheepishly admits.

"Good, 'cuz I know this great pizza joint." We both laugh.

"Let me call my dad on my cell and tell him I will be having pizza with you tonight. You sure your mom won't mind?" Sonya asks with concern. I give no answer. "Dad's around here somewhere, but this will be quicker," Sonya's words trail off.

"Hey, Shorty!" the familiar salutation I had come to dread.

Sonya, still on the keypad dialing her dad, and I found ourselves turning at the same time, coming face to face with T.J. and a handful of followers. Sonya's relaxed expression changes in an instant as she pushes the final button on her keypad with force, but doesn't lift the phone to her ear.

"Looks like Shorty's got himself a girlfriend," T.J. sneers.

"Yep, well she **is** a girl," I counter. "And, keep her out of this."

T.J. signals his gorillas and two of them grab me roughly by my arms.

"Seems Shorty here really likes Little Miss Spicy Pizza Girl," T.J. purrs as he walks up real close to Sonya fingering the gold and red-stoned heart-shaped locket, dangling from her neck. The five bullies all laugh, as I struggle to get away and one of them punches me in the gut.

"Yes Sir, this is some nice stuff you got here, Shorty," T.J. continues without let up, staring directly into Sonya's eyes with nasty intent.

"Way too nice for a creep like you!" Sonya counters with disgust.

With a jerk of his wrist, T.J. snaps the chain holding the gold locket in place. Sonya gasps and grabs for her neck where only seconds before the locket had been hanging. Her eyes fill with tears as she keeps her hand on the spot where the locket should be. T.J. dangles it for all to see.

"Looking for this, Little Miss Spicy Pizza Girl?" he snarls.

Suddenly, a clatter echoes from the other end of the alley. T.J. peers into the darkening shadows of the alley leading away from the arena. He stands stunned and unbelieving, as Joe emerges from the shadowy service area. Joe's eyes pierce T.J.'s with an unwavering dislike. He watches from a distance not taking his eyes off T.J. He is juggling a puck on the end of a hockey stick.

"Oh, well if it isn't Pizza Joe," T.J. announces with confidence. His merry band laughs at the swagger he is demonstrating for everyone's enjoyment.

"Let them go," comes Joe's direct command, with no hesitation whatever.

"Why don't you come and make me, Old Man?" T.J.'s arrogant and disrespectful retort.

"Do you know that a hockey puck is so hard that it could actually be used as a weapon?" Joe poses his cool, calm, quiet question to T.J.

"And what is that supposed to mean?" T.J. asks with disdain. With one fluid motion, Joe fires off the puck at T.J. hitting him directly in the groin. T.J.'s knees buckle and he collapses on the ground, clutching his privates.

"Aargh!" T.J. is unable to form any words and remains on the ground rolling in pain, while his pack watches him with concern. No laughing now.

After many minutes, T.J. rises slowly to his feet. He then grabs the hockey stick laying across my bag and uses it forcefully to drop me to the ground. My nose is a red gusher! I'm in a world of hurt.

"You're next, old man!" T.J. snarls with contempt. T.J. and his pals start to close in on Joe as he stands alone at the end of the alley. He never moves. He stands his ground against T.J.

A huge ruckus erupts as the exit doors in the back of the arena open and the alley fills with suited up hockey players all thumping their hockey sticks on the concrete. A constant Thump! Thump! Thump! Silence meets the appearance of the Detroit Ice Dragons, with their game faces on, determined to win this contest. The goalie drops his helmet's protective mask over his face, and slams his hockey stick on the ground for effect.

"Is it Captain Crunch time, Coach?" the Ice Dragons'

goalie growls, directing his question to Joe, but keeping his eyes squarely on T.J.'s throng.

Still on the ground, but kneeling now, with my nose bleed subsiding, I am astonished to see T.J. and his ring of delinquents back-peddle in retreat. T.J. turns surveying the situation. He is clearly outnumbered, with nothing close to hockey sticks for use, in an all-out street fight. He spins around to make his escape, with his gang on his heels, and smacks right into Officer Bernie Scagliotti, in his police uniform, with his still holstered gun clearly visible. The Ice Dragons walk forward as a group and form a circle around the small group of guys T.J. regards as his personal wolf pack. The Ice Dragons hold their sticks with two hands, just waiting for one of T.J.'s dogs to make a move. They anticipate dishing out the type of high sticking T.J. just used on me. They have my back, and I know it.

Bernie casts a long hard look at the group of soon to be arrested thugs standing before him, and very matter-of-factly states, "I've already called for back-up. Hear those sirens coming, those are **my** guys! And with the Ice Dragons here standing firm, I wouldn't do anything stupid if I were you." Every Ice Dragon holds their position without blinking, glaring right back, stare for stare, at each and every member of T.J.'s pack. There is no mistaking the intent if any member of T.J.'s gang tries to run.

"So, Big Brother are these the bullies you watched wipe the sidewalk with Anthony and James, a week or so ago?" Bernie asks Joe as he stares straight at T.J. without blinking. T.J.'s knees buckle, but he remains standing, as he hangs his head in defeat.

"Yep, the very same ones, Little Brother," Joe answers walking up to stand beside his brother. "Guess you thought nobody else was around to see you carry out your nasty little ambush…oops! Wrong again," he smiles sarcastically at T.J. "And I'll testify to that in a court of law, Mr. I think you'll get to watch me," Joe finishes with his arms crossed in front of him resting across his chest and satisfaction showing on his face. T.J. on the other hand wasn't looking nearly as content.

The back-up, for which Officer Scagliotti radioed, arrive on the scene momentarily. Four officers get out of their police cruisers and walk toward the crowd. There will be no escape from this show-down for T.J. and his horde. The officers start slapping on the handcuffs. It is Bernie 'the Badge' Scagliotti having the last say this time, "It appears you boys will be spending some time in the penalty box," he smiles as T.J. and his gang are loaded into multiple police cruisers for their transport to the city jail, and their own personal time out!

CHAPTER SEVENTEEN

om arrives as the police cruisers are pulling away with lights flashing and the sirens blaring, heading for the police station only two miles away. And of course, the results of T.J.'s handiwork is hard to miss. I am sure my nose is broken. Mom dissolves into tears. Joe is trying to calm her down with the details of what had happened and how everything would be all right. I wasn't even sure I believed what Joe was peddling, but she was reassured for the moment.

Sonya comes walking up to me with my gear bag in hand, holding it out for me to take. She looks at me with an expression I haven't seen before. This street brawl scared both of us. Her concern surprises me. She visibly cringes when I lift the towel I am holding and show her my nose.

"Ouch! That's gonna leave a mark! So sorry, Anthony," she moans.

Joe makes the suggestion that we all go to the pizzeria for pizza on the house, and Mom reluctantly agrees, as she continues fussing about my broken nose. Bernie can't make it for pizza on account of having to fill out all the police paperwork on the arrest just made charging T.J. and his gang with intent to do great bodily harm. It looks as though most of them will be off the streets for a good long while.

Mom and Joe sit in the booth behind Sonya, Vinnie, and me.

"Three meat pizza, my favorite," Sonya says between bites as she scarfs down a slice of pizza.

"Who doesn't like a…hat trick?" I grin and then wince from the smile that stretches my bruised, puffy eye, and my somewhat crooked nose.

"Now you're starting to look like a real hockey player," Vinnie offers with enthusiasm. "Just sorry it had to be from a jerk like T.J. instead of in a real game," he adds.

"This was a real game, Vinnie! The game of life, as we know it!" Sonya was getting all worked up again, "T.J. came out the loser on this one! Well, relatively speaking," she joked looking right at me.

I touch my swollen eye, "Ya' think?" I grab another piece of three meat pizza, with one hand and hold an ice pack to my eye with the other.

"Dad said that was real smart of you leaving your cell phone on speaker, Sonya. That's how we all knew you two were in trouble and needed help," Vinnie offers with pride in his voice. "Dad heard everything on the phone, when you put the call in to him, and he called for back-up right away," he finishes with a pat on her back. I look at Sonya with surprise.

"What?" she counters.

"You even thought to do that?" I ask in complete disbelief.

"Well, thought I should do something to change the odds for winning such a lopsided match-up. Besides, I felt obliged to make up for earlier when I was bossing you around on the ice, teaching you the slap shot routine. I'm only like that when hockey is the subject of conversation," Sonya smirks. "I love hockey and I hate to see it played badly," her final tease directed at me.

"Yah, that's why she makes such a great bench warmer for our Ice Dragons. Sonya breathes fire when things don't suit her," Vinnie smiles with a wink and sticks his tongue out at his sister.

"How about figure skating? Do you love that, too?" I persist.

"Sometimes I feel like it brings me closer to Mom," Sonya looks at Vinnie and he nods in understanding.

Sonya reaches up and places her hand up to her neck, where her gold-shaped, red-stoned locket used to be. Sonya sighs and her eyes start to fill with tears.

"And now it's gone," she confirms in a quivery voice.

"Really? You sure it's gone?" I ask with sincerity.

"Quite sure. I looked, but couldn't find it anywhere. Even some of the guys on the team helped me look for it," Sonya finishes sadly.

I stood up from the booth, "Do me a favor. Stand up."

Sonya rises slowly with a question in her eyes.

I continue, "Now turn around." Sonya turns around. My final command, "Stand still, now." I stand behind her and slide the necklace around her neck. She clutches the locket with a knowing smile, and gives me a quick kiss on the cheek.

"Wow!" She clasps the locket again. "I don't believe it! Thank you, Anthony. Thank you so much! This means the world to me, because it was my mother's," Sonya finishes with tears spilling down her cheeks. She makes a quick exit to the restroom.

"Girls! They always have to go and get mushy about stuff!" Vinnie complains. "Want another slice of pizza? Doesn't get better than hot Hat Trick Pizza!" It hurt to chew, so I decline and watch Vinnie devour another piece.

By the time Sonya comes back from the bathroom, her face isn't splotchy anymore, and Vinnie has moved to Joe's and Mom's table to finish eating the pizza they couldn't. Sonya and I are sitting alone in our booth.

"Anthony, thanks again so much for finding my necklace. I will always be grateful for this," Sonya promises with conviction.

I reach deep into my jacket pocket and pull out the photo of my dad that I had found in the treasure box from the basement. I had kept it in my jacket since the day I found it. I wasn't sure why I did that. I shake those thoughts from my mind, and hand the photo to Sonya.

"It's my father's high school senior picture. People say I look like him," I blurt out unexpectedly. "What do you think?" I ask, because her opinion suddenly matters to me for some reason.

Sonya eyes the photo. She looks at me, then looks down at the photo, and looks back at me again. "You do look like him," she offers, and tries to manage a weak smile. I don't smile, not even a little. I lean back against the booth and let some of the pain wash over me. True to the promise I made to myself, there are no tears in my eyes.

"Can I ask you a question?" she inquires quietly with a mutual sense of compassion in her tone. As I nod yes, she proceeds to ask me the same question I had asked her about her mother, "So, what happened, Anthony? How did your father get shot?"

"He and my uncle went to the corner store to get candles for my birthday cake, and he never came home," I answer the question sarcastically, take the photo of my dad from Sonya's hand and shove it back into my pocket.

"They tried to rob a sporting goods store. The owner shot my dad," I finish, feeling the tears about to come to my eyes. I sure don't want Sonya to see me cry like a little girl, so I continue talking to keep the tears away, "My dad had lost his job, but I never thought he'd rob a store for any reason."

Sonya looks at me. I look at her. Sadness shows in both our eyes.

"I gotta' go," I say quickly, rising from the booth. "I'll see ya' at the game." I walk over to where Mom and Joe are sitting and talking quietly.

"Ma, I'll see ya' at home. I'm walking from here. Won't have to worry about T.J. for a while. Thanks for the pizza, Joe." I leave the pizzeria feeling the eyes of Vinnie, Mom, Joe and Sonya burning a hole in my back, but no one says a word. There is nothing to say. I need some space.

Final Season Game

On Saturday I arrive at the ice arena with James, Mom and Nana. We are there a half hour before the game is to start. I drag my bag of equipment into the locker room. Some of the guys are already here. This is the final game of the season, so most of the teams' families will be here to cheer on the team. Mom, Aunt Cayleen and Nana had announced they were not missing the game, so I was to be sure and get the tickets. James has been badgering me all week so that I would not leave him out. Nana promises to be pleasant and not yell at the refs. Mom and Aunt Cayleen will probably have to hold her to that vow. With James there as my moral support and third greatest fan, I am ready!

Joe paces back and forth like a jungle cat, while the team is wrapping their hockey sticks, and finishing other pre-game prep.

"Well gentlemen, this is our last regular season game before the playoffs, so just go out there and have some fun," Joe shoots us all a toothy, silver-capped smile. "Oh, but make sure we win!" he finishes with humor. We all laugh, but we are serious about getting this win in the books.

"Five minutes to ice time!" Bernie yells out at the locker room door. We all stand up on our blade guards, gather our gear into our bags and head for the door. We walk out together to our bench behind the boards. Both teams of players and coaches take the ice. Each team keeps to their own end of the ice rink, running through the pre-game warm-up drills as practiced hundreds of times. I am nervous with a bad case of the 'butterflies'. I know the feeling is shared by others on my team and the competition.

The horn blares. The teams line up at center ice. I am playing center, so I ready myself for the opening face-off. All the things I had heard my coaches and Sonya say are running through my head. I watch the ref, anticipating

the drop of the puck. I lose the face-off, but play has
begun. The teams go back and forth. I have the puck but
it is too quickly and easily stolen from me. I am feeling
anger rising, discouraged about my poor play so far in the
game. I skate back down the ice, trying to keep my head
in the game. The second period begins. This time, I gain
control of the opening face-off. I move down the ice on a
breakaway. I wind up and shoot, but whiff completely as
the puck glides away harmlessly on its own. A defending
player secures the puck and starts back the other way. The
game is not going well for the Ice Dragons at the moment.

Third period begins. The game is winding down. The
scoreboard reads Visitors 1, Home 1. We are defending
well, but the shots are not falling as we had hoped they
would. The crowd cheers wildly on both sides as the
clock is ticking off the final minute of the game. The
Dragons are on an offensive rush. I am controlling the
puck, moving down the ice fast. I stop short, spot an open
teammate and pass him the puck. An opponent quickly
skates in and intercepts my clumsy pass. Suddenly the
puck is moving in the opposite direction toward our goal
net. The scoreboard is ticking, five…four…three… the
opposing player has a clear breakaway at the Dragon's
goal. He shoots, scores. The horn blows as the time
expires.

The Scoreboard: Visitors-2, Home-1.

The opposing team celebrates their victory. On the
Dragons' bench, some players drop their heads, others
shake theirs. Bernie pounds the rail, Joe simply looks
on. The mood in the locker room is gloomy. The players

quickly change into their street clothes without much conversation. Most have already left. I sit alone at my locker, not wanting to talk or get dressed. I slam my equipment into my duffle bag, kicking my locker and throwing my towel.

A couple of Dragons are leaving the locker room, neither look my way, but give a wave to Joe, "See ya', Coach."

Joe nods to his players. "Get some rest guys. We're going to need you fresh for the playoffs!" After today's game, all the guys feel like a win in the playoffs is like reaching for the stars.

I am alone in the locker room with Joe, still filling my bag with gear. Joe walks over to me, "Ya' know, Anthony ya' really didn't do too bad out there." I slam my bag down on the floor in anger.

"Too bad?! Are you serious? I lost the game for us!" I snarl.

"Oh really? So, you're the only player on this team now?" Joe argues.

"No, I'm just the only player who passes to the wrong team!"

"For crying out loud, Anthony, it was your first real game."

"Yah, my first game," I say with disdain shoving the last of my stuff in the bag. "And my last game!" Silence follows from both sides of this argument.

"So uh, what exactly is that supposed to mean?" Joe presses.

I stand up and sling my bag over my shoulder. "You know what it means. I'm done. D-o-n-e, done!" I spell out as I walk to the locker room exit, turning my back on Joe. "I should have followed my gut and stuck with basketball," I storm, knowing Joe is watching me as I walk away.

I exit out of the arena and into the parking lot. Mom has gone to get the car. Nana and Aunt Cayleen walked to the car with her. I am glad that I'm not having to face them just yet. Only James had waited by the door for me to come out. He knows I don't want to talk, good friends are like that.

"Next time, it's in the win column. You really played better than you think, Shooter," James offers his only comment with a shove to my shoulder.

I don't want to talk about the game, not now, not ever! I was a major disaster out there. I lost the game for my team, and everyone knew it.

"Hey, Anthony! Wait up!" Sonya calls from the back exit. She jogs over to catch up with me, "You looked pretty good out there today."

"Good?! More like horrible to the 10th power!" I declare.

"Seriously, you weren't that bad, Shooter," James argues feebly.

"Just stay out of this one, James! I stunk up the place!" I yell.

"Don't sweat it. There's always the next game," Sonya attempts to encourage.

"Not for me. I'm done with this sport!" I retort.

Sonya suddenly becomes angry, "Just like that, you're done?!"

"Yah, just like that," I mimic her.

"Oh really? So you decide after one meaningless game that this is not for you?" Sonya continues her defensive banter.

"That's right!" I stop and answer, looking directly at her.

"What were you expecting, Anthony? Someone was just going to hand you a pair of skates and a hockey stick and you'd become a star?" Sonya blows out an exasperated breath. "Did you really think it was that easy?"

"What does it matter what I think? I'm quitting!" comes my final reply.

"And so, you're just walking away..." Sonya stares at me with disbelief and disappointment showing in her eyes. "From Joe, from the team, and from me," Sonya glances back over her shoulder as she turns to leave, "I'm sure your dad would be very proud of you!" she bursts out with disgust.

I look at James in amazement, raising my hands in the air and shaking my head. He shoves his hands into his jeans' pockets, shrugs his shoulders, and whispers, "Go figure... girls."

I shout out after Sonya, "I never asked for this! It wasn't part of the deal! I only have to work at the pizzeria until the debt is paid," every excuse I give falls on deaf ears. It is clear that Sonya isn't listening. She will never understand. Besides what does it matter? I never asked to be her friend. I just want to pay off the debt and be done with the whole thing!

CHAPTER EIGHTEEN

Sunday was going to be a long day. I am still not talking about the game that I lost for my team on Saturday. I didn't really even feel like getting out of bed. But it was church... every Sunday, rain or shine. I can hear Mom calling down the stairs for me, "Anthony, twenty minutes before we leave for church. Get yourself up here, and you best be looking like you washed behind your ears and your clothes didn't come out of a laundry basket settin' around for years. This is the second time I've called you," Mom ranted.

"Yes, Ma'am. I'll be ready shortly," I yell from my room as I scramble out of bed. I run up the stairs, into the bathroom to throw water on my face, brush my teeth and comb my hair. I'm doing a mental check of what exactly I will pull out of my closet to wear. *No wrinkles or spots. A tough one! Black pants, good shoes, gray sweater and socks. That'll do.*

I arrive upstairs at the front door with only minutes to spare. Nana had stayed the night and begins giving me the usual once over: Checking my ears, turning me around to see if the creases in my pant legs are holding their press enough. She never neglects to let me know if anything is amiss. This is no different, regardless of how bad I am feeling about losing the game yesterday. She never 'walks on eggs' when it comes to doing things right.

"Son, those shoes need a buff with the shoe cloth. Go along to the kitchen and get that attended to. Ya' know, ya' can't be goin' into the Lord's House looking like ya' don't care a whit 'bout your appearance!"

I run through the kitchen door to grab the shoe cloth out of the broom closet and almost slam into Mom coming out of the kitchen.

"Slow down, Anthony! You 'bout ran me over!"

"Have to buff my shoes before we leave, Nana's orders."

"Be quick about it then and get in the car," Mom dictates over her shoulder.

We all arrive to church on time, looking good in our Sunday best. The Reverend keeps it short this Sunday, probably 'cuz the Detroit Lions are playing at 1:00 against the Chicago Bears and it is sure to be a beautiful day for football. Reverend Case does love his Lions. I'm trying to stay focused on the Reverend's sermon, but I keep going over the bad pass that caused us to lose the game. My mood is not the best, though church has a way of improving my outlook in general. By the time the service is over I feel better. I am determined to forget about the game and look forward.

We are in the car backing out of the church parking lot. Mom is driving. Nana is saying what a wonderful sermon the Reverend had given, inspiring so many people in the congregation. Then out of the blue…

"Anthony, your uncle wants to speak to you," comes Nana's bombshell.

"Not now, Nana," I protest though ever so politely.

"Yes, now!" Nana states emphatically.

I do not want to hear this, and I sure don't want to do what she is suggesting.

"But...," I begin.

"Don't you 'but' me!" Nana orders not backing down. "You will do as you are told. This has gone on long enough! You're going 'cuz **I** say so and your mother agrees!"

I know not to push any further.

On the drive home from church, I am riding in the backseat, sullen and silent. Mom stops at a store that sells flowers, located between the church and home, and comes out with a bouquet.

"You got flowers for Uncle Alonzo?!" I ask incredulously.

Mom turns to me with annoyance showing in her eyes, "They are for your father's grave."

I turn my head away like I could care less, and add nonchalantly, "Why? He's dead. What good are flowers goin' to do him?"

"He may be dead, but his spirit will always live on," Nana assures followed by a short scripture recitation. Mom drives into the cemetery and stops the car on the road a few feet from the grave.

"Anthony, come and pay your respects to your father's grave," Mom begs for compliance.

"I will not, so please leave me alone about it," comes my stubborn refusal. *Man, what a day this is turning into!*

I watch as Mom and Nana get out of the car, and Mom carefully lays the fresh bouquet on the gravesite, at the base of the headstone. They stand holding hands, saying a quiet prayer together. I can see my father's name carved clearly in the finished stone, but the rest of the headstone is hard to read because of the size of the letters. Nana and Mom are partially blocking my view anyway. Suddenly, without warning the tears spring to my eyes. I can't stop their coming. I fight them back with all my will, but still they keep coming. I kick the back of the car seat and stare out the side window, letting the tears fall. I wipe all traces of tears from my face before Mom and Nana come back to the car.

After leaving the cemetery, we pick up Aunt Cayleen and begin the drive to the state prison in Jackson where Uncle Alonzo has been transported to serve out his sentence. Aunt Cayleen sits in the back with me. I am mad at being forced to see my uncle. I stare out the car window so that I don't have to talk to or look at anyone. No one is talking much. I ride in sullen silence the rest of the way there.

We arrive about an hour and a half later. It is the first time I have ever seen a big state prison. The facility is huge! I see rolled barbed wire fencing around and on top of the high fenced wall that marks the perimeter of the prison area. They call it a Maximum Security Prison. We get checked at the door. The guards show us into a visiting room with tables and chairs.

I sit with my arms folded across my chest a few chairs away from everyone else in the room. My legs are stubbornly stretched out in front of me with my ankles crossed. I lean back in my chair, with my eyes closed. I am defiant and unapproachable because I do not want to be here. I am feeling something uncomfortable in the pit of my stomach. All the way here I have been imagining what I will say, when I finally see my uncle again for the first time since that awful day. I feel guilty because even though I am furiously mad at him, I wish it was my dad I am about to see, not my uncle.

The guard who directed us into this family visitation room suddenly opens the door on the opposite wall. I can't help opening my eyes to see what is going on here. Uncle Alonzo, dressed in a prison uniform, enters into the visiting area. He approaches and hugs Aunt Cayleen, and nods with lowered eyes to Mom and Nana. Though they greet him, Nana and Mom keep their distance from Uncle Alonzo.

"Anthony," my uncle calls to me from where he has just greeted Aunt Cayleen.

I turn my head away as Alonzo walks over and holds out his hand for a shake. I keep my arms folded.

"Your mom told me you're playing ice hockey," he tries.

I turn to my mother with anger showing on my face, for the fact that she is discussing any part of my life with Uncle Alonzo. I say nothing.

"How are the new inlines working out for you?" I ignore his question, even though he is standing in front of me. I don't look at him.

"All that street skating you've done must come in handy playing hockey," Uncle Alonzo continues trying to find a way to open the door with me.

At this point, I can stand it no longer and bolt out of my chair.

"Really, I've heard enough!" I shout starting to leave.

Uncle Alonzo grabs my arm firmly.

"I don't want to talk to you!" I shout.

The officers start to intercede with Uncle Alonzo. He lets go of my arm and puts his hands into the air to show he means no harm, then holds up his hand to stop them from taking him out of the room.

"Listen to me, Anthony!" Uncle Alonzo thunders with anger that matches my own. "Your dad didn't rob Sammy's Store, I did!" my eyes lock with his.

I want to believe what he is telling me is the truth, but I don't trust him. I turn my face away; angry beyond words.

"Believe me, Anthony! Your dad had no idea what I was up to. He was just an innocent bystander," Uncle Alonzo pleads for me to believe him. An officer stands on each side of him, holding onto his arms.

"You're lying!" I shout, shaking my head 'No'.

"No, I'm not!" Uncle Alonzo forcefully defends.

"Why did you wait until now to say something?" I accuse as my eyes fill with tears, and a black hole of hate rises inside of me.

Uncle Alonzo lets out a big sigh, "I've wanted to tell you, but you wouldn't come to see me," he argues his case.

"You couldn't have told Mom or Nana?!" I continue the interrogation with a combative edge.

"I needed you to look me in the eyes and know I am telling you the truth," my uncle continues pleading with me for reason. "I love you, Anthony. I don't want you to live another day thinking your dad committed a crime. It was me, not him!" my uncle broke down.

He slumped into a chair nearby where the officers had guided him and sobbed with his head on the table between us. He composed himself after a few minutes. No one was showing him any sympathy.

My uncle remained at the table, but would not stop trying to convince me of his story, "Your dad wanted to buy you a real basketball hoop with a glass backboard for your birthday. You know, it had been weeks since we had work. We were both low on money. Instead, he had gotten you a table hockey game from one of Gramps old buddies. It was practically brand new, still in the box. He and your mom had agreed on that gift, and could better afford it."

At this point, Uncle Alonzo is becoming more agitated and starts pacing back and forth in front of the table with his head down looking at the floor. He begins continuing on in a way that seems like he is talking more to himself than to anyone in the room, "But no, I wanted more for you, Anthony. I wanted you to have the real thing 'cuz I knew you'd love it! Besides why shouldn't you have what you want, you're a great kid?" my uncle continues explaining, defending, and sharing his remorse.

Our broken family listens intently to his explanation and confession of guilt. Aunt Cayleen is crying. I am helpless to move.

Uncle Alonzo continues, "At the last minute, I insist that we go to a second-hand sporting goods store where I'd heard you could get great deals. Your dad insists we just go to price a used hoop. Well, the guy at Sammy's Sporting Goods store wasn't dealing that day! Even a used backboard with a hoop was more than your dad or I could swing, so Tom goes back to the truck to leave. He said how you'd be disappointed with the hockey table game, but he figured it would be better than gettin' no gift at all." Uncle

Alonzo looks at me and sees the tears running down my face. "It was me, Anthony! Me insistin' we needed that basketball hoop and backboard," he continues to plead. "Your dad was well out of it. Then he came back into the storage barn wonderin' what was keepin' me. I had my hands on Ole' Sammy, and we was fightin' over the gun. That was when it all started going so wrong! It should have been me that got shot, not him! Your dad was tryin' to stop me!" my uncle finishes spilling the details of a nightmare that won't quit.

At this point mom starts crying and yelling at Uncle Alonzo, "Why didn't you just leave it alone, Lonzo? Why didn't you just let things be?!" she voices the questions and accusations we all carry around in our hearts and minds every day. "Now, my Tom's dead, and our family is broken!"

"I wish I could take it all back. I wish I was dead, not him! I might as well be! Michele, Anthony, please forgive me?!" my uncle is begging, clearly distraught. The guards begin moving forward to restrain him.

I can't stand listening to my uncle's confession or see him like this one minute longer! I don't want any of us to have to endure one more second of pain from his words. The tears which I had fought for so long came gushing out. Whether from relief of finally knowing the truth about my dad's innocence or the extreme force of holding them in for weeks, there was no stopping this flood of my tears.

I storm out of the visiting room yelling over my shoulder, "I will never forgive you! My dad is dead because of you!" I can hear my uncle shouting my name as the door slams behind me.

It is a quiet drive home. I stare out the window with tears rolling down my cheeks, dripping off my chin, wetting my t-shirt. My heart and mind are trying to make sense of what I've just learned from my uncle. Mom and Nana glance at each other a few times, but no one says a word out loud. Aunt Cayleen sits looking out the other window. I know she is crying, too. I reach into my jacket pocket and pull out the tattered high school picture of my dad, retrieved from the treasure box. His image is there looking back at me through the photo as I wipe tears from my face. *How could I have judged you so unfairly, Dad? How could I have not known the truth, somewhere deep in my heart, about your part in all of it? I should have trusted in you.*

The journey back home finally ends. It is dark. Mom has dropped off Nana and Aunt Cayleen, and pulls in the driveway to park the car in the garage. I am exhausted, like I'd just played two hard games of hockey in a row, yet I'd only been riding in the car for a few hours. I can tell that Mom is exhausted, too. Here's another day that I will never forget: The day I found out that my dad wasn't a thief. He had not robbed the store after all, and everything he taught me about being good and doing right is part of who he really is; *then, now, always.*

I walk down the stairs to my room. Mom and I had quickly and quietly said our 'Good Nights', with a promise to talk about all of it in the morning. Mom had shared that maybe it was best for both of us to sleep on it for tonight. The events of the day were running through my head, from beginning to end. The moving picture just would not stop.

I flop down on my bed with all my clothes on. I feel tired but I'm wide awake. Uncle Alonzo's admission of truth had released my father from the guilt of crime he had been accused of, and I had believed was his. It was a relief beyond anything I had ever felt before, when I knew for sure, that what my uncle had told me was fact. The anger and feelings of betrayal, which I had carried around about my dad, are gone. I once again feel proud of my father, just as I always had before this whole nightmare started. Dad had tried to do his best to make my birthday happy for me. He had done the right thing in getting me the hockey table. In some ways it had lead me to a place where I would never have gone on my own.

I remember the torn picture; thrown in the bottom drawer of my desk when Mom and I had disagreed only a few days after Dad was killed. I get up from my bed and go to the bottom drawer of my desk. The picture frame, with the other half of the torn photo, is still there face down in the bottom of the drawer. I pull both items out, and grab tape from my desk. I take the torn off half of the photo and with the greatest of care tape the two parts back together so exactly, that now, you can barely see that it had ever been torn. I look with satisfaction at the restored picture. Dad and I are side by side again, back in the frame as we had been; me and Dad looking out from a wonderful day together.

I put the picture frame back on my desk where it had set for all the days before my birthday. It is back in exactly the same place, where Mom would see it, and perhaps find some comfort in the care I had taken to repair it. I knew this was a very small way of saying how sorry I was for not believing in my father.

Somehow I had to find a way to make it up to Dad for not believing in him and for not knowing in my heart that he would or could never do something like rob a store: No matter how it may have appeared to police. Mom believed that he didn't do it. She had kept saying that this was a mistake, her husband would never do something like that. I had to find a way to make it up to Dad and Mom, so they would know I was sorry for not believing in what my dad had stood for all along.

CHAPTER NINETEEN

Playoffs

Ice Dragons vs. Mohawks

*M*om dropped me off at the door of the Mohawk's ice arena. We were running a bit late. This arena is clear across town on the east side near the Canadian border. Mom had gotten tied up in traffic getting back from Aunt Cayleen's house picking up Nana. I was late meeting the rest of the team at Joe's for the ride across town, so now I'm on my own hurrying into the hockey arena. Mom and Nana are parking the car and finding their seats while I get ready for the big game.

I struggle into the locker room carrying my bag of hockey gear over my shoulder. The bag feels heavier than usual today. I am probably still feeling the effects of all I had heard a few days before about what really happened with my dad. I get my gear on as quickly as I can and walk on my blade guards out to the bench with my hockey stick in hand. I notice the new jerseys everyone else has on, but make no comment. I still have on my old one.

Joe looks up when I come in, but keeps up his pep talk

to the guys. I don't make eye-contact with him, I just sit down and listen to his words.

"Remember, you're a team. And that is your strength. Look out for yourselves and each other," Joe draws a breath, as all the guys on the team look at me, including Sonya who has just joined the bench for the pre-game pep talk. "You got that?" everyone looks back at Joe and nods.

"Yes, Coach!" the team answers in unison.

"Bring it in," Joe shoots out his hand, the team stands and extends their hands, "On three then," the team places their hands on top of his. The last hand to top the pile is mine, with Sonya's just beneath.

"One…two…three…" Joe counts the familiar chant.

"Ice Dragons!!" everyone shouts in unison.

The team leaves the locker room to take the ice for warm-ups. Streaming out into the arena is impressive, with new shiny hockey jerseys, no longer wearing our raggedy practice uniforms. Instead, everyone but me has on the tournament silver and black team jerseys with my original logo of the Ice Dragon on the front and each player's name and number on the back. Joe shoots out his arm to block my way, "Hold up a minute there, Anthony." Joe digs into an equipment bag and pulls another jersey out. He tosses it to me. He hesitates, "Wasn't sure this one was coming out of the bag. Glad you're here, Anthony." I look down embarrassed.

"Oh, I almost forgot," Joe adds holding up his finger as if to remind himself.

"What's that, Coach?" I ask with confusion as I pull on my new jersey with the coolest dragon I had ever drawn adorning the front. I have to admit to myself… *It is awesome!*

Joe reaches into his pocket and pulls out a piece of paper. When he opens it, I recognize at once what he holds in his hand. It is the I.O.U. that has bound us together for several months now. Joe rips it into little pieces.

"Paid in full. No more child labor, and you still have a job at the pizzeria if you want it. It is up to you," he reaches out to shake my hand.

"One more thing, Brooks…," Joe reaches into the equipment bag, where the new tournament jerseys had been stashed, and pulls out a miniature hockey player similar to the ones James and I had been playing with at home from my own table hockey game. "Thought you might like this game piece that your dad used when he and I played a game or two of table hockey together years ago. He always wanted this guy to be his player. I still have the game, so just thought you might like it, too." Joe laid a small miniature player in my hand with the same jersey number on the shirt as the number printed on mine. "Your dad, he was pretty good. Beat me a time or two at table hockey, and never let me forget it," Joe smiled.

"Thanks, Coach" I stammer with emotion. "Thanks for everything. I'm not mad at you anymore," I finish with a smile and offer a handshake.

"You got it kid! Now go out there, be a Dragon and breathe some fire!" Joe concludes by slapping me on the back for emphasis.

The warm-ups commence and soon the game is on!

I take the opening face-off again. The referee drops the puck. I'm not letting it go this time! I win the face-off and the Dragons quickly set up in the offensive zone. The puck gets passed back to me. I see the opening and take the slap shot. Like a bullet, the puck zooms to the goal. The goalie makes a great save denying me the goal and the first team score. The game goes back and forth for most of the first period the game remains tied: Zero to zero.

The second period begins with great effort and speed by both teams. I steal a pass near center ice. I spot a teammate on a breakaway in great position. I pass him the puck in near perfect form. The Dragon takes the shot, but it clanks against the crossbar. No goal! Play continues back and forth, back and forth. Neither team is giving up a score.

Third period begins. Still zero to zero, and everyone is getting edgy on both benches. Frustration is clearly etched on every face. The Mohawks' action is fast and a lot more physical in the third period than the Dragons expected. Some of the checking gets the whistle, but a lot of it just goes uncalled. It is getting rough, and tempers are flaring. I take the puck moving through the Mohawks' defense with speed and agility. I make a hard even stroke of my stick and tuck it into the corner of the Mohawks' net. Score one for the Dragons! I skate around behind the goalie and net pumping my fist in the air. The Dragons' fans erupt! The team piles up into joyous celebration. The Dragons' bench, including Sonya, celebrates their first playoff win!

Scoreboard: Ice Dragons-1, Mohawks-0 Final!

It is back to Joe's after the game and another post-game pizza treat on the house. I am getting used to this and it feels great! After we all have our pizza, Joe walks over to the team chalkboard and crosses off the defeated Mohawks. Mom and Nana are sharing in the glow of the win once again, and would not hear of leaving Joe's without paying something for the pizza everyone was enjoying.

"We have to get going and take Mr. Big Shot home to bed. **Big** game in only two days, you know!" Mom chirps cheerily to Joe.

Sonya and Vinnie look at me with a smirk. "Awww… got to get home and get yer' beauty sleep, Mr. Big Shot?" Vinnie mimics for effect.

"Yah, well don't you lose any sleep over me getting enough," I tease back smiling at Sonya.

"Okay, see you tomorrow then," Sonya laughs and so do I.

"Hey, Brooks wouldn't want to deny you any shut-eye coming up on our big game, in two days!" Vinnie continues to tease.

"Thanks. I'll be ready. You can count on that!" I promise as we head out the door for home and a good night's rest.

It is going to be a big game for sure! It will be the Ice Dragons versus the Bandits. James begged a ride to the game with us. He is getting more and more into hockey. He loves hanging out with the Ice Dragons. He asks almost daily if we can play the hockey game I got for my birthday.

We play as often as we can, and still get our homework done. It is getting harder to beat each other, because we have both improved our strategies for winning.

After school on Monday, I shared with James about visiting Uncle Alonzo and what he'd had to say to me about my dad.

"Never doubted your dad for an instant, Shooter. My dad said there was no way your dad would be a party to somethin' like that, and he was right," James smiles with confidence.

"You told me I wasn't seeing things straight. I was so mad at the world I didn't know what to believe. But you still believed that the true story had not yet been told. Thanks for that, James and thanks for being my best friend and putting up with me lately!" I beam as I slap him on the back.

How right James and Mr. Whitely were, and how relieved I was that it was so. I'm a lucky guy to have a friend like James. He did know my dad well, and for James to believe, even when I didn't, maybe he knew him even better than me. I am still feeling low about being so negative about my father for so long. It's been hard on Mom. I have to find a way to make it up to her and my dad. The question is how?

Ice Dragons vs. Bandits

The game is on. Warm-ups end as the crowd rises for the National Anthem. James and Mom wave to me from the stands. Nana raises her cowbell for me to see she is prepared to use it. James follows with a high five from ten rows up. It makes me smile and I relax a bit.

This playoff game is at the Bandits home rink. We drove about 35 minutes to get here. It is an impressive arena. One of the nicer ones we've played in. It will be a tough game to win. The Bandits hold many of the records in our junior league and are an aggressive team.

I zoom over to center ice to take the face-off and start the game. I manage to get the puck and quickly move against a wall of Bandit defenders. I swing behind the net, curl around the corner and then spot an open teammate rushing the goal. I pass it off, straight and forcefully, my teammate gets control and takes a quick and hard slap shot. Score!

Joe, Bernie, Vinnie, and Sonya jump to their feet. They can't believe what they've just seen. The Dragons swarm each other.

Scoreboard: Visitors-1, Home-0. The game continues with the Bandits determined that the Dragons will not score again. The play goes back and forth, both teams fighting hard for a win. Almost at the end of the second period, the Bandits score with a long driving shot from center ice. A play we weren't expecting and neglected defending. Scoreboard at intermission: Visitors-1, Home-1.

Third period continues much as the rest of the game had gone. Back and forth, back and forth with scoring attempts blocked at every turn on both sides. Finally we are getting down to the closing minutes of the game. Joe calls a time out and we gather near the bench.

"Dragons, this is the time to pull out all the stops! We have to set up the plays faster and with more precision. You can do this, now get out there and breathe some fire!

On three…," all hands pile on, "One, two, three…,"Joe counts.

"Go Dragons!" the team shouts with confidence.

Tempers had been flaring due to the intensity of the game. One of the Bandits lost it on a denied pass that got physical with no foul called. He used his stick illegally and was called for unsportsmanlike conduct, sending him to the penalty box. A power play was just what we needed. With only two minutes left to play in the game, we all knew this was our big chance.

We start from center ice, passing the puck back and forth. They'd capture it, we'd get it back. Then suddenly, one of the Dragons takes a great steal from an opposing Bandit player. An honorable mention Dragon player, Kevin Miller from last year's season, sends a straight pass across the ice to the corner shooter who passes it to the forward in front of the net. Swish and Slap! Score! The Dragons go crazy with only forty seconds left to play in the game. We hold off the offensive drive and the buzzer sounds!

The Scoreboard: Ice Dragons-2, Bandits-1. Final!

Two hours later the team arrives back on our side of town. Every one cheers as the Ice Dragons enter Joe's Pizzeria and fill up the empty seating. Sonya had texted the game's outcome to the other workers ahead of our entrance. Coach Scagliotti is enjoying the love. He walks over to the team chalkboard and crosses off the defeated Bandits. We all cheer and bang on the table tops.

"Okay, okay you guys. We are making progress! Let's

see if you're ready for the Really Big Show! You know the Chippers have a reputation like no other team we have played yet this year. They are tough. They are big. They are ready to win it all!" Joe warns with seriousness. "Well, so are we!!" I respond with enthusiasm. All my teammates stand up extending their arms toward each other at chest level as if laying on the hands, "One…two…three…," I shout.

"Go Dragons!" everyone in the pizza house joins in the chant, as all arms go up, and wiggling fingertips reach toward the ceiling.

The next afternoon in the basement, James and I continue our own personal vendetta squeezing in another game of table hockey. James doesn't stop talking about our real hockey win against the Bandits. He loves every aspect of the game more and more. Our on-going battle at the table hockey game keeps us enthused about the real sport even more. James loves being a part of all the excitement. Basketball has suddenly taken a backseat to hockey for James, but only for the moment.

At home, things are starting to feel a little more bearable. The hockey thing is keeping all of us focused on something other than Dad not being around. James and I spend as much time as possible hanging out, but between school, work, and hockey, neither of us are enjoying much spare time. Still, James and I take every opportunity possible to go after it, just for fun, in the table hockey playoff tournament we have organized between us. I beat James soundly the first two games. He promises to get me next time. We both spend a few minutes every game arguing over which of us gets to be the team whose center's name we have christened 'Captain Crunch'.

Dragons' players and fans alike are getting pumped for the upcoming game against The Chippers. Everyone seems to be in a hockey state of mind. Many people coming into the pizzeria are talking about the game, and asking questions about The Ice Dragons and our recent successes. Even with all this going on, school still comes first in my family. James and I are finishing our evening study session for the unit history test we will have in class on Friday. We decide to squeeze in a quick table hockey tournament game during our 'break' time from studying. The game is the Ice Dragons vs. the Chippers, of course. I make James be the Chippers. Captain Crunch is of course on the Dragon's team for the miniature tournament.

After about twenty minutes of play, James humbly acknowledges his defeat at the hockey table tonight and concedes, "I have to say, Shooter you have become one impressive hockey player. Who would have guessed that 'Mr. Big Shot' would end up on the end of a hockey stick, making his "big shots" on skates and slamming a goal into a net waist high?" James smiles and shakes his head, "Being a spectator at your games, suits me just fine, but it sure can be exhausting! This hockey thing is beating me down, thanks to you! Basketball is my game." James gives me a sly wink.

James starts gathering his things quickly. He's getting ready to head home, mostly in response to his mother's cell phone call, only moments before, reminding him it is still a school night. I'm standing at the end of the hall and watching James' back disappear up the stairs as he heads for home. I'm hoping the game against the Chippers is as easy a win as the game I just finished with James. I know it won't be.

I'm still thinking about the table ice hockey game we just finished. Suddenly, a thought comes to me. I quickly return to my room and grab a black magic marker from the top drawer of my desk. I pop off the cap on my way to the backroom and the hockey table. I bend over the table and darken the face of the center. He now stands out clearly as a black player among all the other white hockey players displayed there on "the ice". I stand looking at my work and smile for the second time in a long, long while.

Ice Dragons vs. The Chippers

Finally Friday night arrives. The week has dragged on and on. Nana, Aunt Cayleen, Mom and James will be cheering me on from the stands. I have been nervous most of the day. It is difficult focusing on much of anything related to school. I keep running over and over in my head another new play that Sonya had taught me. We practiced relentlessly for days. I am hoping that when the pressure is on, I can pull it off when it really counts and add up another score for the Ice Dragons. This playoff game is going to be a show stopper!

The first period is almost over. Try as we might, we don't score and neither do our opponents. The battle rages on, back and forth between the Chippers and the Dragons. The Ice Dragons have the puck down near the Chippers' goal. There is a wild skirmish. The Chippers' goalie gets drawn out. The puck squirts to the side. I am there in position and slap the puck into the open goal. The team roars as I pump my fists in victory!

After my goal, we seem to catch fire and start 'breathing fire' into each other on the ice. The Chippers are struggling to keep up with us and perhaps for the first time in the season, the Dragons can see fear in their opponents' eyes. The Chippers are playing to keep from losing instead of playing to win! The Ice Dragons take the lead and skate into the finals!!

The Scoreboard: Ice Dragons-5, Chippers-1 Final!

The drive home after the game was non-stop talking. Nana has the most to say about how the Ice Dragons 'whopped those Chippers'! Every game she has come to see, she makes sure her cowbell rings out her support for what is happening on the ice. James is really loving hockey tournament action. Hockey is proving to be a sporting event that is pulling us all together in ways we had never dreamed. The ice between Sonya, Vinnie, Joe, Bernie, and I has melted.

The next day I walk into the pizzeria reporting for work. I see the team chalkboard marked, *"Playoff Bracket."* Joe has crossed out the defeated Chippers. I love seeing the line drawn through the Chipper's team name, announcing silently their defeat by the Ice Dragons. Hockey is feeling like my sport after all.

I am spending a lot of time practicing. Tonight is no different. Sonya and I ride over to the arena with Joe. He wants us to practice some skill drills that she had taught me a couple of weeks before. Coach is sitting in the bottom row of bleachers as Sonya skates onto the ice, with me following behind. Sonya's pads and mask are off and she turns to face me with her hockey stick pressing into my chest, holding me at a distance.

"I have a new move for ya'," she smiles.

"What kind of move?" I ask with my eyebrows raised and a smirk on my face.

"Not that kind of move," she pokes her stick at my chest again. "Here let me show you," Sonya takes the puck behind the goal as if sweeping to the other side, but then reverses quickly into a figure skating rotation before skating to the left red line circle and shooting the puck for a goal.

"I thought we were supposed to practice the drills you taught me two weeks ago? Besides, this is hockey, not figure skating," I complain.

"Which is exactly what the Bladesmen won't be expecting," she counters.

Sonya steps aside to let me practice the move. I try it many times in succession; all of them unsuccessful. The first time, I don't reverse hard enough and go down on my rear. The second time, I reverse okay, but in the spin-rotation, I lose the puck at the end of my stick and it flies into the sideboard. Every time something doesn't work, I get more and more frustrated, despite Sonya's patient and encouraging words. Finally, I cut too close to the goal, clip my skates against the frame and go spinning off. I turn on the goal and bash the top of the frame with my stick. The stick splinters and breaks.

"Aargh!" I scream at the top of my lungs. Sonya skates

quickly over to where I am bent over from the waist with my head in my gloves.

"Hey, hey…easy does it," she says in a soothing voice.

"I can't do this!" I say with frustration in a loud tone.

"Yes, you can, Anthony. I know it," she persists.

"We're playing the Bladesmen in two days," I argue, as I skate away from her. Sonya reaches out and grabs my jersey spinning me around to face her. She looks hard into my eyes without blinking.

"Forget the Bladesmen, forget hockey! What's bothering you? Why are you so angry?" she insists without letting go of my jersey.

I let out a long breath of air before I blurt out, "My dad, he wasn't there for me on my birthday… and he won't be in the stands with my mom and Nana watching me play. He won't ever be there! Don't you get it?!"

"I'll be there," Sonya says softly as she hugs me around the neck.

I turn around to see if Joe has seen our exchange. He sits there smiling his shiny, silver-toothed grin. I shrug my shoulders with a straight face, and raise my eyebrows. I can hear Joe laughing.

CHAPTER TWENTY

The Final Game

The Ice Dragons vs. The Bladesmen

The Final Game day arrives bright and early. I can't stay in bed one more minute and I'm up earlier than usual, sitting in the kitchen having a bowl of Captain Crunch cereal. Mom has made a point of buying this earlier in the week, due to the featured photo of Mr. hockey power, tough guy, Wendell Clark, on the front of the box. His claim to fame was his stick-on handle mustaches and his nickname 'Captain Crunch' given for his pounding style with a hockey stick and puck. One of Joe's favorite hockey personalities! Mom had made me promise to wait until game day to eat the cereal. Well, it's game day and I am digging into it now! I'm totally staring at the 'Captain Crunch' cereal box photo when Mom walks in, still in her slippers and robe.

"Well, I see you have the day off to a good start. What on earth are you doing up so early, Mr. Big Shot?" she inquires, yawning as she reaches into the cupboard for a bowl.

"Looks like I should be asking you the same question," I grin back.

"How's the Captain Crunch?" she asks, not pausing to answer my question to her. "The big game starts at 7:00 p.m.! You ready to breathe some fire?" Mom teases with a smile. "Anthony, your dad would be so proud of the way you have developed over the last few months. He would love to see you play hockey," she adds on a more serious note. I could see the tears starting.

"It's not basketball, Mom. Dad always wanted me to play basketball," I remind her.

"Anthony, it was never about basketball, or any specific sport. It was about you becoming the best you can be. It has always been about you. Your father loved you very much. Dad never meant for this to happen to any of us," she finishes with tears streaming down her cheeks.

I stand up from the table. "I know that now, Mom. I'm just so sorry that I didn't trust who he really was. I don't know how to make up for not believing in Dad the way I should have. I'm so sorry for making this worse for you," I hug her tight. I hate it when my mom cries.

"There is nothing to forgive, Shooter. Dad knows you are sorry, and so do I. He is always with you, no matter where you are. I hope you believe that," Mom holds me at arms-length to look in my eyes, so I will know she means it.

"I really want to, Mom, I really do."

It is finally 6:00 p.m.; pre-game time, and one hour before face-off, as Mom pulls into the parking lot of the Scagliotti Ice Arena. Nana, James, Aunt Cayleen, and Mom are all in the car, coming to the game to cheer the

Ice Dragons to a victory. They all chatter on the ride across town, but I'm not feeling like talking much. *Home team…Final game…Gotta' win…* keeps running through my brain. Mom pulls up near the back door of the arena. Only James and I get out now and walk the twenty feet to the back entrance, while Mom parks the car.

"Hey, good-luck now, Shooter. You gotta' take these guys. Don't let up on them for a minute. Make those shots strong and straight. If they get sloppy, make 'em pay! We've got the home advantage!" James encourages.

"Gonna' do my best, James. This is the biggest game I've ever played. Hope all the practice and slave labor pays off!" I smile as we part ways. I walk into the locker room to tape up and get ready for the game. James waits at the back arena door for Mom and the rest of my family to appear.

A few of the other guys have arrived early as well. We are quiet, sorting through our bags, pulling out our equipment. We are all lost in our own thoughts as silently we tape our sticks. Soon we are chatting again, putting on our gear, and greeting teammates as they come through the door to suit up. After donning all my hockey gear and putting on my Ice Dragon jersey, I gather up my street clothes to put them in my bag. I flip my jacket off the bench and the high school picture of my dad flutters from the pocket. I reach down and pick it up from the floor. I sit there looking into the eyes of my father, who is looking back at me from the tattered picture.

I can hear Dad's words echoing in my head. "Trust in yourself! Never give up! Remember, Shooter: Once a hero, always a hero."

It is as if he were giving me the pep talk that would have come had he still been alive. I put the picture back in the jacket pocket and shove the jacket into my bag. I wish so much that he could be here tonight. I guess he is here in ways I am finding hard to understand.

All is relatively low key until Coach Joe bursts into the locker room about ten minutes before we are to take the ice for warm-ups.

"Gather 'round, Dragons," Joe orders. We all swarm around him. "I want you to look at this dragon," He proudly points to the Ice Dragon embroidered on the front of his coach's jersey, the very one I had designed. "Dragons: Symbols of power: Formidable opponents," Joe limps back and forth in front of his team. "It's a fire breathing dragon ready to strike with power, confidence and strength," Joe never flinches. He's on a roll now with the motivation speech. "And strength comes from confidence in trusting in yourself and your team," Joe clasps his hands together. "Now go out there and play with all you've got, no matter what happens!"

Joe sticks out his hand, every player adds to the stack, "On three! One…! Two…!Three…!" when the last hand tops the pile, we all shout, "Ice Dragons!"

We hobble out into the arena on our blade guards. The crowd on our side goes wild! Everyone is cheering, some people, lining the sides of the hall, slap us on the back until the last Ice Dragon is away from the crowd, cutting circles and lines on the ice. The arena is packed with spectators. We begin our pre-game warm-ups with excitement and determination. I hear the cowbell clanging, and look up to see Nana waving her arms, ringing her cowbell, and smiling like it is Christmas. She is standing in the bleachers seven rows up, between Mom and James. James has his hands over his ears. I guess Nana is overdoing it with the cowbell! I can't help smiling to myself. *I guess she has gotten over the fear of me having my teeth knocked out!*

My teammates and I are grabbing quick glances at the Bladesmen as they run through their pre-game drills. Some of them are very big, and very fast*! How can I not be nervous watching these guys skate around like they have been doing it since they learned to walk?! No time for this.*

The referees skate out to the middle of the rink, at center ice. A whistle blows. The starting six of the Ice Dragons head onto the ice. The two players taking the face-off shake hands. The referee drops the puck, and the game is on!

First Period, the Ice Dragons get possession, but quickly lose it. An opposing Bladesmen takes the puck, moves swiftly across the red line, the blue line, dodging, swerving. He passes across to a teammate, who slaps it toward the goal. The Dragon's goalie catches it, and holds the puck aloft for all to see that he has made the save. The crowd cheers loudly! Back in play again. Quickly an opposing player steals the puck, then passes it to a teammate who tucks it into the net past our goalie.

The Scoreboard: Bladesmen-1, Ice Dragons-0.

Play resumes, starting the Second Period. The Ice Dragons have possession and are moving the puck well. I am feeding it down the sideline, close to the boards, when an opposing player checks me into the glass. The crowd

207

boos, but no whistle. A Bladesmen scoops up the loose puck and passes it down to a teammate toward our goal. He fires from twenty feet out. The Dragons' goalie blocks it, but a Bladesmen is there to fight for it. Another Dragon gets into it as well, but again, an opposing player sneaks up, steals the puck and scores.

The crowd is completely engrossed, and watches as the competitiveness between the two teams increases to new levels on the ice. Play is getting rough and some players are pushing the lines with cheap shots. I get mad, come back with a vengeance, making a great pass to a Dragon teammate and we score! I skate away, fist pumping our first goal. The opposing team's goalie shrugs it off, putting his mask back on.

The Ice Dragons' bench goes wild with cheering and jumping around. I hear Nana's cowbell clanging. I look in the direction of the sound and see Mom, Nana, Aunt Cayleen and James cheering from the bleachers. Sonya raises a drink bottle from the bench and squirts it into the air. I smile.

As play resumes, the opposing team comes out with faces set in determination. Moving toward the Dragons' goal, a Bladesmen gets the puck stolen from him. My Dragon teammates cheer my steal. He doesn't like it one bit! I pass it off, but an opposing player comes back at me, from behind, and checks me so hard, my helmet flies off and down I go, spinning in circles, on the ice. Everyone sees it, including the ref. The crowd boos angrily, including the Ice Dragons' cheering section.

The opposing player is sent to the penalty box. He steps into the box with a scowl. Clearly he is not happy about the call he has just been given. A power play begins with a vengeance. The Ice Dragons circle the goal and take shot after shot, but can't put it in. Finally, an opposing player gets the puck on an errant pass, and in a superb three-on-two break manages to score just as the buzzer sounds at the end of the second period.

The Scoreboard: Bladesmen-3, Ice Dragons-1.

It's half time, and players on both teams head to the locker rooms. The Dragons welcome the break. Joe limps in and stops in the middle of the room. Our team huddles at the benches. Sonya hands out water bottles. All the players are quiet waiting for Joe's words.

"Look guys, we've been outplayed in every aspect of this game," Joe scolds. We hang our heads looking and feeling dejected. "They're more physical. They're stealing passes left and right. If it wasn't for Jason's goal tending, we'd be getting crushed right now!" Joe pauses momentarily after this second criticism. Each player is intent on what's coming next.

"But, we're still in this. One good pass. One good shot. Maybe a lucky break and ..." Joe pounds his fist into his palm. "Bam!" the team suddenly comes to life inspired by Joe and his positive ways to inspire. "This game is **ours**! Every dragon guards and protects its lair!" he concludes with authority. The players all rise, circling our coach. Joe commands an answer, "Can we do this?"

"Yes, Coach!" we all shout with conviction.

Joe sticks his hand out. "Bring it in, Dragons,"

everyone puts their hands in the middle. "One...Two... Three...," Joe counts robotically.

"Go Ice Dragons!" we all shout to the rafters.

The ref skates to center ice with the puck, about to start the third period of the Championship Final. I get the face-off spot going against an opposing Bladesmen. Not a word is spoken. The ref drops the puck. The opposing player gets it, passes it back to his teammate. A Dragon steals it, passes it to me and I skate away with it. The crowd cheers! There is a certain amount of back and forth until the Dragons get into a wild scramble in front of the Bladesmens' goal, trying to pass the puck around and get a score. An opposing player hooks me with his hockey stick...hard! Down I go onto the ice. The ref doesn't see it. Another Dragon falls on top of me and pushes the loose puck into the net. Score Dragons! The home team and crowd goes crazy! *Wasn't pretty, but we'll take it!*

The Scoreboard: Bladesmen-3, Ice Dragons-2.

As I'm lying on the ice gathering myself after the hook, I can hear Mom's voice yelling out above all the others, "C'mon ref!" I feel faint and am seeing stars for a second. I look toward Mom's voice, and think my eyes are playing tricks on me. For an instant I believe I see my dad sitting behind my mother. I shake the image out of my head and struggle to get up. I scramble to get back into the mix.

The other team's player takes the puck and drives straight at our goalie. He shoots from ten feet out. Jason blocks it, but the puck slides away from him. He leaps forward and smothers it. Nice save! A Dragon takes the puck after winning the ensuing face-off and passes it down the side to me. I make a sharp cut to the inside completely beating my defender. I speed forward unopposed toward a Bladesmens' guard. I put a move on him, and shoot! Miss! Hits the frame of the net and glances off.

In the following face-off I get the puck, and pass it back to another Dragon before any Bladesmen can trip me again. The opposing team player, on a bad pass, kicks it over to a Dragon, and back to me. The opposing team player steals it. I steal it back, charge the goal and pass to another teammate who's right beside the net. My teammate makes a swipe at the puck with his stick, completely misses it, and the puck hits his skate, rebounding to me. I am ready. I crush the puck into the net and score! I fist pump, "Yes-s!" The crowd shrieks and claps.

The scoreboard: Bladesmen-3, Ice Dragons-3.

Over on the Dragons' bench, Joe, Bernie, Vinnie and Sonya are all smiles. In the stands, Nana rattles the cowbell and whoops and shrieks, attracting amused attention from the crowd.

"We want…" Nana shouts. "M-o-r-e goals!" she cheers clanging her cowbell even louder.

Back on the ice, I steal the puck from a Bladesmen offensive player and break away. Just as I close in for the goal, one of my skate blades snaps off and I totally wipe out! I hear gasps from the crowd, as I hurl toward the ice. The side of my face slams against the ice. I glimpse Mom covering her eyes, afraid to look in my direction. Nana stands with her hands on her hips, and concern etched across her face. A whistle blasts! The ref skates to a stop beside me, ice chips flying.

"Time Out!" he yells. Joe and Bernie scuttle across the ice and approach my sprawled out body. They are both kneeling beside me in an instant.

Joe calls out my name, "Hey, Anthony…Hey, Anthony… You all right?"

I feel disoriented for the second time that game. "Huh?" I stammer.

"Are you hurt?" Joe questions with concern, checking for dilated eyes. Bernie is giving me a once over checking for cuts or broken bones. There are none, so he turns me over on my back with Coach's help.

"Uhhh…naw, I don't think so," I say with uncertainty. I look up at the steel beams across the ceiling rafters and they seem to be moving back and forth. Joe and Bernie help me to get up on my feet. I brush myself off, and try to gain my balance. The dizziness is easing up. Joe and Bernie help me to the bench, hobbling all the way, with one skate blade on and one skate blade off. I plop down on the bench. The refs continue clocking the full time-out for my injury. Bernie quickly unlaces the broken skate and pulls it from my foot. Coach, is looking at my pupils again to see if they have dilated.

"Sure there's nothing broken? Joe asks with concern.

"Just a skate," Bernie quips as he raises up my busted skate looking at it with dismay. "Unfortunately, it's the only one that fits his foot."

Joe bolts from the bench, disappearing into the locker room. Moments later, he emerges with his old Red Wings duffle bag. He pulls out a pair of well-used skates with slightly rusty blades. "These'll do!" Joe announces.

The ref blows the whistle for play to resume. The Dragons take the ice. I'm on the bench getting this equipment problem resolved.

"Whose skates are these?" I ask with curiosity, as my head begins to clear. I can feel Joe and Bernie pulling another pair of socks over my own. Joe slides the battered skates on my feet and, with fingers flying, begins lacing them up.

"Oh, these belong to some old pizza guy who loves the game of hockey," Joe teases. He looks up and winks, "It's Captain Crunch time!"

I fly back onto the ice feeling 'The Force' of the Red Wings under my feet. The Ice Dragons have been back on the ice for only one minute and fifteen seconds after the short timeout. I am more determined than ever, that nothing is going to stop me, or get in my way for bringing home this win.

A Bladesmen is next to me in a flash. He crouches for a big attack. I zoom in at the last second and block the opposing player into the boards, as we struggle for possession of the puck. I whiz over and steal the puck from him, then blaze like lightning the entire length of the ice with an opposing player chasing me all the way, swinging his stick out after me but unable to catch up.

The crowd starts chanting, "Dragons!... Dragons!"

The scoreboard is ticking off the seconds: ten... nine..... I am a good skater, but the three guys after me are just as good. Suddenly, I take the puck behind the goal as if sweeping to the other side, but then reverse quickly making a figure skating rotation, just the way Sonya and I had practiced it. I slide in an instant to the left red line circle and position myself like the cutout player on my table hockey game. I pull my arm back with even shoulders about to slap shot the puck with all of my strength.

Instantly, I hear my father's voice in my ear saying, "Trust yourself!" I shoot the puck, driving it so hard it practically tears a hole in the net scoring the winning goal. The buzzer sounds! The audience goes wild!

Scoreboard: Ice Dragons-4, Bladesmen-3. Final!

I throw my hockey stick and raise my arms to the ceiling in triumph! On the bench Joe, Bernie, Vinnie, and Sonya are hugging and jumping around. I glance over at the bleachers to check Mom's reaction and am stunned to see again, a ghostly image of my dad there between Mom and James, as my family stands cheering to the top of their lungs for me and the Ice Dragons.

I can see James shouting, "Shooter! Shooter!" But my focus is on my father's presence there. *He hadn't missed it after all.*

Suddenly they are all lost to my sight when I'm instantly mobbed by my teammates creating a pile of Ice Dragons celebrating in front of our opponents' goal. There is no time for further thought on the matter. My teammates rise from the ice, pulling me in every direction, and hoist me up over their heads in victory! They skate as one wave of Ice Dragons around the arena holding me up for all to see. The bleachers have completely emptied out and everyone has rushed the ice to celebrate our victory. As I am being skated around on display by my teammates, I'm straining to look toward the stands where I thought I had seen my dad. But no, the image is nowhere to be seen. It was only an instant, but I knew he had been here.

The Dragons lower me back down on the ice... carefully. I slowly turn to find myself face-to-face with Sonya wearing a big smile on her face, and clutching a squirt bottle in her hand, which she proceeds to empty over my head. We are both laughing, and enjoying the victory celebration.

"Way to go, Mr. Big Shot! I just knew that you could do that move!" Sonya beams, throwing her arms around me and hugging me tight. I hug her back, as she places a kiss directly on my left cheek: Making today one of the best days of my life, and it wasn't even my birthday.

"Thanks for teaching me how to figure skate," I smile.

"Thanks for finding my mother's necklace," she smiles back. "And I love the drawing you did of me skating my triple spin," I look at her with shock. "Fell out of your bag at the T.J. scrimmage. Have it framed in my room," she smiles and hugs me again. I don't even care that she'd found it.

The celebration at Joe's pizzeria was the best yet. Even some of the regular customers had heard the news and showed up to pass the hat and treat everyone on the team and their families to pizza. With spirits running high, I work up enough nerve to ask Sonya if she wants to come over to my house and watch a movie until her Uncle Joe picks her up after he closes the pizzeria. She didn't say no.

During the celebration of our victory over the

215

Bladesmen, Joe makes a great display out of standing up on a chair to cross out the last opponent's name on the Playoff Bracket Chart, The Bladesmen. Only the Ice Dragons' name remains at the very top of the bracket. It brings the house down and everyone claps and cheers for too many minutes to count.

It is late by the time we leave the pizza house. Joe is coming by our house later to pick up Sonya after he closes up for the night. Bernie has to work the midnight shift, so he is depending on his brother, Joe, to be his daughter's final ride home after a long, but exciting day. On the way back from the pizzeria, Mom drops off James, Aunt Cayleen, and Nana. Only Mom, Sonya, and I are left in the car when my mother pulls away from Nana's house.

I ask Mom if we can drive by the cemetery so I can visit Dad's grave. It took no persuading to get her to agree, despite the late hour. Sonya responds to my request with a warm knowing smile and a quick hand squeeze to show her support.

"We'll wait in the car, Anthony," Mom offers.

"I won't be long," I promise.

I open the car door and walk into the darkness of the night. The lights from the streets surrounding the city cemetery shine on the path enough for me to easily find my way to the spot. The ground, still too freshly dug, feels soft and squishy under my shoes. I hate that part. A lump starts to rise in my throat. I approach my dad's headstone. Digging into my pocket I pull out the miniature hockey player from my table hockey game; Dad's birthday gift to me. The black face I had fashioned with a permanent marker was still clearly visible. 'Captain

Crunch' has become my good luck charm for playing hockey successfully in the last two games. I kneel down and stick the player into the ground at the base of my dad's headstone, just beneath his name and mine.

Thomas Anthony Brooks
Loving Husband and Father
"Once a hero, always a hero"
(1973-2009)

I stay on my knees in the soft grass, saying my words aloud.

"I love you, Dad. I'm sorry for thinking the worst about you. I'm asking you to forgive me. I hope you like the way I played hockey for you tonight. I knew you were there. I wish you were here. You will always be my hero," I finish softly, no longer fighting the tears, and not caring who knew.

I stand, and turn away slowly. I walk toward the car meeting Sonya half way. She had left the backseat of the car to meet me when she could see that I was on my walk back from Dad's grave. She reaches out and takes my hand smiling knowingly. We walk silently back to the car together.

ABOUT THE AUTHOR

BRIAN WEBSTER

Brian is an "Idea Man". He has turned his ideas into several screenplays, two of which won awards at the Moondance International Film Festival and another finalist finish in a Holiday Screenplay contest. He has coauthored two adult books, *Death by Default and Bundle of Hope*. His children's books include: *Snowville, Santa's Elf, Trapped in Toyland, Model Kid* and *Recipe for a Monster. Monkey Flip and Comic Detective* are Brian's two previous Young Adult Readers. Brian enjoyed coaching youth athletic teams when his sons were young. Brian lives with his wife, Cathy, in Canton, MI. Together they travel across the country to visit their five adult children and two granddaughters.

TERESA LEE

Teresa Lee (Schanski) has authored two children's chapter books: *Boxcar Joe, (2012)* and *Leggins (2014)*. Teresa presented for The Michigan Reading Association at the 2013 summer conference on Mackinac Island. She has presented at a host of MI schools as a featured March is Reading Month author. Teresa has recently written her first adult novel, *As the Willow Bends*. Her life has been greatly enriched through a long line of very serious and accomplished family sportsmen: Athletes, coaches, and sport enthusiasts. Black Ice is her first collaborative effort at turning a screenplay into a quality Young Adult Reader. Teresa lives in Perry, MI with her husband, David, and enjoys the love of a very large family and nine amazing grandchildren.

Printed in the United States
By Bookmasters

Printed in the United States
By Bookmasters